ICE & BERRIES

LEAH R CUTTER

KNOTTED ROAD PRESS

Reviews
It's true. Reviews help me sell more books. If you've enjoyed this story, please consider leaving a review of it on your favorite site.

Come someplace new…
Do you enjoy exploring strange new worlds, new cultures, new people? Sign up for my newsletter and I'll start you on your travels with a free copy of my book, *The Island Sampler*.

http://www.LeahCutter.com/newsletter/

Buy More!
Did you know that you can buy directly from the Knotted Road Press website?

https://www.knottedroadpress.com/shop/

ALSO BY LEAH R CUTTER

Cozy Fantasy

A Dragon's Guide to Killing Gods (And Other Lies)

Epic Fantasy Series

The Fallen Elves

Ruins of the Gods

Stairs of the Gods

Cities of the Gods

Graves of the Gods

Forgotten Gods

A Wind Blown Torment

A Stone Strewn Clash

A Sea Washed Victory

The Tanesh Empire Trilogy

The Glass Magician

The Desert Heart

The Ghost Dog

Houses of the Dead

Houses Divided

Houses Fallen

Houses Reborn

The Clockwork Fairy Kingdom

The Maker, the Teacher, and the Monster

The Dwarven Wars

The Chronicles of Franklin

Franklin Versus The Popcorn Thief

Franklin Versus The Soul Thief

Franklin Versus The Child Thief

Mysteries

The Water Witch Cozy Paranormal Mysteries

The Witch is Inn

To Scratch a Witch

Witches and Waterways

Grilled Sand and Witches

The Lake Hope Cozy Mysteries

The Purloined Letter Opener

The Tell Tale Heart Pin

The Halley Brown PI Mysteries

Dancer in Darkness

Trophy Hunters

Collections

The Alvin Goodfellow Case Files

The Rabbit Mysteries

The Shredded Veil Mysteries

CHAPTER ONE

Elbriarien stood her ground as the giant ice demon rushed towards her and the other two Ice Elves standing on either side of her. The three of them struggled to hold the monster back in the wintry maelstrom. They'd used a major spell to create the net-like barrier that held back the beast, and its blue ice magic glowed strongly in the swirling snow. However, the net dimmed every time the beast threw itself at it.

Pellets of sleet abraded Elbriarien's cheeks. Shrieking winds as well as the demon's howls scoured her ears. Elbriarien used a cantrip—a tiny bit of magic that came naturally to the Ice Elves to keep her body warm, as the bitter cold was harsh enough to freeze a Human in place.

The three Ice Elves couldn't hold the demon in place for much longer. Even the protective shields they had each spelled into being wouldn't save them.

Behind Elbriarien hulked a giant war machine of Dwarvish manufacture. It generated a steady stream of ice and snow that the Elves controlled. The storm it created was more natural than the magical cold manifested by the demon. The three Elves gathered the machine-generated cold and directed it, driving back the unnatural winds and sleet.

Fighting ice with ice.

This latest demon attack had started further south than usual. Not quite properly into the territory claimed by the Ice Elves, but close enough that Elbriarien could possibly visit her parents, as it would only take a few days to get to her home city from this location, instead of the months it took from the usual front line.

The ice demon raged at the Elves standing in its way, roaring with fury, the beast intent on claiming this area as is own. It pushed toward them, desperate to dig in and force its frost into the earth, ensuring that the ground wouldn't melt again, not even in Elbriarien's lifetime.

It was actually a good sign that the demons had grown so desperate as to encroach on land this far south, places that would see a summer, albeit short. It meant that the demons' own territory was growing crowded, that the Elves had been successful at keeping the demons from expanding further.

In addition, there had been fewer attacks during this past year than in the previous decades. The demons might eventually be defeated. The elders had grown hopeful that the Great Mistake, the awful spell which had brought the ice demons into the world of Annund in the first place, was finally weakening.

Elbriarien planned to prove herself to her master with this latest battle. She needed to earn the title of Ice Mage so she could make her way in the world. Maybe she could travel south, out of the frozen lands and see the sights that the bard Gytha had told her of.

No one would hire a mere apprentice. Not anywhere,

north or south. No matter how talented she might be. Plus, the King's Law said that anyone who wasn't a Mage or a Master couldn't use magical spells. Cantrips, yes. Spells, no. At least not by themselves, without the guidance of a Mage.

It wasn't a popular law, but magical communities—particularly the Elves—ruthlessly enforced it.

It had been an Elf who hadn't worked his way up to Mage who'd caused the Great Mistake in the first place. He'd been trying to create a magical portal. He hadn't had the training to control the spell, and the demons had hijacked it. It continued running, five hundred years later.

While Elbriarien's companions held the attention of the demon and kept it at bay, she cast her next spell, aiming it at the war machine, getting it to belch out a large amount of ice and snow. She sent the huge ball straight up instead of attacking with it.

In a few moments the barrage of ice and snow from the war machine abated. She could finally see the ice demon with her eyes.

Like most of its kind, it had the head of an eagle, with white feathers, a yellow beak, and glaring golden eyes.

However, the head by itself was taller than Elbriarien, who stood a good six foot two.

A long, snaking neck connected the head to a massive four-legged body. The white feathers gave way to silver scales which were imbued with magic and almost impossible to penetrate.

The stout body rippled with muscles. At its shoulders, the beast stood twelve feet tall. Diamond-hard silver talons tipped its claws. A single swipe from one paw could take out an entire house if the creature were allowed into a village.

Instead of wings, it had a mass of black tentacles

streaming from just below its shoulder blades. Each one of those ended with a hard spike, crackling with magic and cold.

Even an Elf wouldn't survive being skewered by one of those.

A barb tipped its tail too, though with a spade-like end that immediately froze whatever it touched.

Elbriarien waited as the creature roared its challenge at her, its golden eyes focused on the prey immediately in front of it. It took a step back, then charged at the net. The blue magic crackled like ice breaking, growing black and weak in spots. The demon bellowed as it struggled, sensing its victory was near, believing that it could break free if it just pushed hard enough.

It didn't notice the two Elves sliding to either side, creeping closer to it in the periphery.

The beast snarled as it eyed Elbriarien, ready to make a final charge. It paused as it gathered itself together.

With a downward motion of her hand, Elbriarien dropped the mass of snow and ice that had been gaining altitude all the while.

The snow thudded down onto the demon, forcing its head to the ground, burying just that part of the monster while the rest of its body remained clear.

The two Elves rushed in from the sides. The most vulnerable location on an ice demon was where the feathers on the head transitioned to scales on the neck. The Elves attacked with spears they had enhanced with ice magic. The black spearheads looked frail but were actually strong enough to shatter stone walls.

Before the demon could free itself from the snow that covered it, the Elves struck, slicing the demon's head from its body.

The storm around Elbriarien instantly abated. Snow started to delicately drift down. The air grew still and hushed. Though it wasn't warm, it was no longer bitterly cold. She took a moment to revel in the natural weather.

"Some help here?" Hangorior said, his tone as dry as the air around them.

"Coming," Elbriarien said, ignoring the part of her that bristled at his words.

A "thank you" would have been nice. Appropriate, even. With her help, they'd been able to dispatch the demon quickly, before they'd had to cast any more magical spells or use any more costly ingredients, like the rare glowing angleworms that they'd used for the net. It wasn't as if she'd been standing there doing nothing the entire battle.

She knew better than to expect appreciation from these two, though.

The three Elves worked together, chanting a spell that created a shield that encased the demon's body, preserving it. Ice Mages had many uses for the magic stored in the remains. Left alone, the ice demon's body would have quickly dissolved into a huge, dense snowbank.

"Nice trick with the ice," Bengaliemin said eventually.

"Thank you," Elbriarien said, glancing pointedly over at Hangorior as the three of them worked together, floating different parts of the shield around the beast.

Hangorior shrugged. "I never thought this plan would work."

"What, you didn't think you could skewer a demon that had been immobilized? Don't be so hard on yourself," Elbriarien teased. "Or were you doubting Bengaliemin's skills?"

That earned her hard glares from both Elves.

Eventually Hangorior said, "I am surprised that you were able to stop a demon by dropping snow on its head."

"Then why let me try it?" Elbriarien asked. "I could have been killed."

Though Elbriarien stomped down on her internal frustration of always being doubted, she knew that her death had always been a possibility. Perhaps the massive amount of snow dropped on the demon's head wouldn't have been enough. Or maybe it wouldn't have landed in the right place and the other Elves wouldn't have been able to skewer the creature's neck. In the worst-case scenario, she wouldn't have dumped the snow and ice in time, and the demon would have killed her before she could have done anything else.

It wasn't as if she could try the move a few times on a practice demon.

"I let you try it because you're the most expendable," Hangorior said with a shrug. "Nothing personal."

Elbriarien kept her sigh to herself. That was the problem with being a mere apprentice. Far too many Elves worked at their craft for centuries and never advanced to being an Ice Mage, let alone becoming a Master Mage. She had a single black magical band around her left wrist, marking her status as an apprentice, unlike Hangorior and Bengaliemin who had two silver bands, showing that they were Ice Mages.

Though Elbriarien knew her odds weren't great, she still believed that a single fifty-year apprenticeship with Dragon Azutjengaban would be sufficient to advance. She wasn't like the other apprentices Azutjengaban had, such as that dullard Daerethel, who'd spent hundreds of years working like a slave for Azutjengaban and never advancing. He'd always hidden in his study, never braving the demons, instead, merely doing research for Azutjengaban.

Surely ending a demon attack as quickly as she had would be the final proof that she was worthy and ready for the title of Ice Mage?

She'd find out next week when she went to visit her master. In the meanwhile, she did the work assigned her, continuing to prove her worth, feeling alone despite her two companions.

The bard Gytha had told Elbriarien of other dragons, who lived in grand palaces filled with gold and decorated with precious gems and beautiful murals.

The dragon Azutjengaban lived in an ice cave. Carved, life-like statues lined the white crystal walls, images of all the peoples: dragons, Elves, Dwarves, Gnomes, and even Humans. They weren't necessarily famous people, or even people Azutjengaban knew, just ones that he found beautiful. They glowed with blue ice magic, staring down with blank eyes at Elbriarien as she walked down the hallway.

Though Elbriarien was inured to the cold, this hallway always gave her the shivers. She gratefully stepped beyond it, and out of those sightless gazes.

Today, Azutjengaban sat in his receiving chamber, on his golden throne. The dragon had taken on a more Elf-like appearance that morning: tall, thin, graceful, with pointed ears and short blond hair.

However, he maintained some dragon features as well, such as his large amber eyes with a vertical pupil, ridges across his brow and down his oversized nose, and two dozen dragon whiskers—each as big around as her thumb— dangling from his chin to mid-chest.

The modest room he greeted her in could hold perhaps six people, who would all stand lower than the raised dais. While the walls were still the same whitish-crystal, the floor had a black stain to it, with gold veins running through it, like frozen marble. Magical fairy lights shone from the corners, giving a shimmer to the walls and floor.

"Ah, my apprentice!" Azutjengaban's voice boomed through the room, echoing off the walls. "Welcome! I've heard of your latest victory!"

"Thank you, Master," Elbriarien said with a bow. "It was a good battle."

"Yes, you have done well for yourself," Azutjengaban said. "And for me. You have had a profitable apprenticeship with me."

"Profitable, Master?" Elbriarien asked.

"Oh, you know, side-wagers, battle betting polls, and the like," Azutjengaban said.

"You're making money off my people dying?" Elbriarien said, trying to keep the shock out of her voice.

"No, no, nothing so crass as that," Azutjengaban assured her. "It has much more to do with my position among my peers. Favors owned and owed. No gold changes hands. That would be crude, even for a dragon."

"All right," Elbriarien said, letting the matter pass. It was never wise to delve too deeply into the finances of dragons.

"I'm assuming you want to continue with me, yes?" Azutjengaban said. Without waiting for an answer, the dragon continued. "There are some new fighting techniques that I'd like to start training you in."

"That's it?" Elbriarien asked, unable to contain her anger.

"What do you mean?" Azutjengaban said, sounding shocked that Elbriarien had interrupted him.

"You won't even consider me for advancement?" Elbriarien said.

Azutjengaban sighed. "Fine. I suppose we can go through the formalities. Apprentice Elbriarien Itamar. Report your work and achievements under my tutelage."

Elbriarien already had her list compiled. She started with her first battles with the ice demons, merely as support staff, and how she'd worked her way up until she was directing the others.

Azutjengaban listened with a bored expression.

"Anything else?" he said when Elbriarien drew to an end. "Any new spells created? New artifacts? Ancient texts translated?"

"No," Elbriarien said quietly. "I've been on the front lines, fighting." The magical nets to contain the demons, the shields the Elves used, though powerful spells, were well known, and she'd cast them with the guidance of the Ice Mages she'd been working with. Even getting the great Dwarven war machine to belch out a large amount of snow and ice at one time wasn't much of a change from the usual spells.

"You should have found time for more than just that," Azutjengaban scolded. "Even Daerethel could have done more. In fact, that's all he does."

Elbriarien blinked, startled.

Then she saw the truth of it.

Daerethel would never advance because Azutjengaban wouldn't allow him to fight demons.

On the other hand, she would never advance because she would always be fighting. Even if the demons were eventually defeated, Azutjengaban would find other battles to throw her into. Other ways to "profit" off her.

"You have decided that I should not advance?" Elbriarien said. Just the words made her feel as though chains weighted down with blocks of ice wrapped around her wrists, hunching her back and drawing her shoulders toward the ground.

"Now, dear, of course you'll advance one day. You're just not ready yet. Really, after only fifty years? You need more patience. That's barely a tenth of your life!"

Elbriarien knew Ice Elves generally lived five hundred years. Some of the elders were closer to eight hundred.

Fifty years might seem like a drop in the bucket after she'd lived longer, but for now, it was all she'd known. Most of her life had been working as an apprentice.

How many centuries had Daerethel been there? Three? Four?

No. She longed to see the world, to visit magical palaces. Experience the ocean. Perhaps even walk without shoes on a warm beach.

She wouldn't be stuck here in the cold forever.

"That is your final word?" Elbriarien said, her tone flat. She couldn't give into the screaming, crying, or even rage that threatened to engulf her.

All that time. All those years.

Wasted.

Azutjengaban's eyes glittered with amusement. "It is," he said, sounding self-satisfied.

"Then I won't waste any more of your time, insisting that you train someone as unworthy as myself," Elbriarien said. She bowed her head, turned, and started walking out of the receiving hall.

"El," Azutjengaban said, his voice resigned.

Elbriarien paused, but didn't look back.

Her left wrist tingled as magic circled it.

Had Azutjengaban changed his mind? Was he going to promote her to Ice Mage anyway?

No. She watched the black band marking her as an apprentice dissolved, leaving no trace behind.

If she wanted to advance, she'd have to go through another apprenticeship, from the start. Give up another fifty years of her life.

Elbriarien nodded at Azutjengaban's decision. He could have left the apprentice mark. Masters usually did when an apprentice left to go study with another Master.

Of course, the dragon wouldn't. They were too selfish in nature. The Bard Gytha had warned her about that as well.

With her head held high, Elbriarien left the ice cave and its magical, glittering statues. Left her former Master. Left the battles behind. All alone, and on her own.

She had the rest of her life to herself, now.

About time she took charge.

CHAPTER TWO

Elbriarien stood on the prow of the sailing ship *The Piebald Pup*, staring across the gray waters. They had finally turned, and instead of heading due south were now going east, along the coast, heading towards her final destination, the city of Osirholm. From where she stood she could see row upon row of terraced neighborhoods rising from the gentle bow of the bay they were about to enter.

She had been traveling for three months now. *The Piebald Pup* had made several stops along the way, giving El time to acclimate to each new environment, the warmth slowly increasing each day.

Every port they'd visited had been a new experience for her. Ice Elves didn't build cities like they did in the south, in warmer climates. They dug into hills and under the earth, living in insulated caves. The cities built by the Ice Elves were beautiful, of course, decorated with magical lights and filled with statues, fountains, and filigree art. They didn't spread out though, or have grand structures. Those were too difficult to build as well as maintain in such a harsh environment.

Osirholm was the largest city on the coast, as well as the southern-most port of the continent of Annund.

Even Llaeno, the grandest of the cities of the Ice Elves, was a quarter of the size of the port towns she'd seen. Ten Llaenos could easily fit on the bottom two tiers of Osirholm.

And there were dozens of additional tiers going up the hill.

"El!" called Captain Masym. "I know yer thinking an old blowhard like meself should have enough hot air to fill those sails on me own. I keep working on it but I can't. Not yet. So some help would be appreciated, if ye don't mind."

Elbriarien blushed and immediately called up winds to fill the sails. Her winds weren't that strong, and she couldn't hold them hour after hour. However, the delicate extra touch she gave to the sails made maneuvering the ship easier whenever they came into a port.

Elven winds and that sort of easy magic, that came naturally to her without having to cast any spell, was classified as a cantrip and could be done without breaking the King's Law.

Plus, helping out with the winds on the ship had meant she hadn't had to pay for her passage. That sort of barter was considered legal for the most part.

While Captain Masym considered it a good bargain, Elbriarien was exceedingly grateful, believing it was the least she could do.

Particularly when it turned out that there really wasn't anything else that El could do on board. She wasn't physically strong enough to help with loading or unloading the cargo. That wasn't how her magic worked.

If the captain had asked for an ice slide to push the cargo down off the ship, she could have obliged, though that would have been less legal, as she'd have had to actually cast a spell to create such a structure.

Levitating heavy cartons straight up and moving them along? Not really something she was good at, even with a spell.

Cooking wasn't her forte either. Her people ate raw fish, pickled greens, and the various mushrooms that they grew in their caves. She had no idea what to do with a frying pan, let alone all the chilies and spices favored by the crew.

It had certainly been an experience for Elbriarien, learning all the new tastes, smells, and textures of food.

Now, though, a different adventure awaited her.

Trying to find her way on land, so far from home.

Her parents hadn't been thrilled by her leaving and heading south. Her mother had (rightly) blamed the bard Gytha with putting so many wild stories into El's head.

Ice Elves stayed in the north. Or at least so she'd been told by everyone, from her aunts and uncles to her youngest cousin and oldest grandparent. Few had ever made it out of the frozen tundra, let alone all the way to Osirholm.

The land here looked alien to Elbriarien. She'd never seen so much green, not even in the summer fields up north. So many colored birds sang to her whenever the ship touched land. So many flowers to smell and spices to try.

And so many different people to see. Humans came in all colors, from as white as she was to ebony black. Dwarves too. The Gnomes tended more toward the orange ends of the spectrum, with untamable white mops for hair. She'd seen a few Gnomes who'd added brilliant blue, green, or even red dye to their wild manes.

The Woodland Elves she'd seen had skin the colors of trees, from pale white to golden brown. She hadn't met an

Umber Elf yet—one whose skin was black with red eyes. They came from over the mountains to the east, and were cave and desert dwellers.

The wind teased El's long chestnut-brown hair. She'd gotten used to wearing it tied in a long braid hanging down her back. The air this far south felt soft against her skin, full of moisture and frequently too hot. Fortunately, the same magic that had kept her warm during demon battles now kept her cool in the heat, as well as protected her skin from the ravages of the sun. She'd exchanged her long, white-wool robes for lighter cotton, though she still wore mainly whites and beiges.

Elbriarien listened to the port as they drew closer: the cries of the fish mongers hawking their wares; gulls complaining of stolen treats; the creak of wooden wheels against cobblestone; a thousand conversations all taking place at once—bargains being haggled, deals being struck.

All those people.

Elbriarien had had to force herself to step off the boat at the first port town the ship had pulled into. She'd never seen such a mass of people, not even during the solstice celebrations of the Ice Elves.

And that had been a tiny town, a village, compared to Osirholm.

Elbriarien stopped looking at the city and focused her attention back on the sails. She had a job to do, so she pushed her winds back and forth, letting the boat tack in place, drawing them slowly into the harbor.

"Pier at the far right," the captain informed her.

El nudged the ship that direction, maintaining the finely aligned push-pull that kept the ship at a constant slow speed. It took a little maneuvering to get them parallel to the dock, but Elbriarien had had enough practice by then to bring them in smoothly, the side of the ship never scraping against the wooden pier.

As sailors started tossing and catching ropes to tie the boat to the pier, Captain Masym came over to chat with El.

"Good work, lass," he said, nodding at her. "I don't see how ye can do all that pushing and pulling such a big ship as *The Piebald Pup*, given that yer as thin as a leaf. But ye do good work. Are ye sure ye don't want to make the trip back? We've had fine sailing with you along. Fine sailing."

The captain, like most of the two dozen folk who made up the crew, was Human. He was younger than Elbriarien, merely in his late fifties while she was closing in on seventy, though she was aware that Human life spans didn't usually go past a hundred and fifty. However, he looked more like an elder, as his wild mass of black curls had huge swaths of silver in it. So did his thick beard. She was certain his eyes had faded, going from dark to a more honeyed brown now. However, they still gleamed with joy. He barely came up to Elbriarien's collar bone and his stocky body was thick with muscles. Like the rest of the crew, he wore a whiteish long-sleeved shirt to keep the sun off, loose black cotton pants, and a floppy hat with a white, tan, and brown bandanna tied around it, representing the ship.

When Elbriarien had first learned the name of the ship, she'd assumed there would be a dog running around on it. It wasn't until their third port of call that she'd seen the seals who'd inspired the ship's name, a particular breed that had sleek black bodies but a piebald face with colored patches all across their snouts.

El had been the only Elf onboard. In addition to the Human crew there were three Gnomes who did most of the cooking, as well as two Dwarves who yelled and swore at anyone who would listen when the seas grew rough. They claimed they couldn't swim and would sink like stones, so the sailors needed to be more careful.

Why they insisted on staying on the ship when they were obviously so afraid, Elbriarien had never understood.

Then again, they did get to bargain at every town the boat stopped in. It was enlightening to watch them. They frequently bragged that they got better prices for the ship's goods than anyone else could. Though El had learned how to bargain as a young child, she'd never seen it developed into such an art form before.

"Thank you Captain, for your kind offer of further employment. And maybe one year I'll take you up on it and sail back. For now, I want to stay here, in the south. To experience constant summer, instead of constant winter."

"Well, we'll be here for a good week or more. If ye stumble, don't hesitate to ask for help. I'm sure we can help ye get back on yer feet, settled out in no time."

"Thank you," Elbriarien said, touched. The captain had looked after her from the start, smoothing over her awkwardness and lack of common experience.

"Ye'll be fine, I'm sure. Ye'll find yer legs and go marching off quick as can be," Captain Masym assured her. "Now, ye remember where I've told ye to go? The name of the inn? And the innkeeper?"

"Yes," Elbriarien said. "To *The Book Ends* inn, up on the third tier, and ask for Nellie."

"She'll help ye end up on yer feet," the captain said. "But if ye have problems, there's still a bunk here. Ye've got a deft hand with the sails, and the crew likes ye, for all yer Elfness."

"I appreciate it," Elbriarien said, understanding that it

had taken the crew some time to adapt to her, and her to them. It warmed her heart to be accepted and welcome, particularly after the way Azutjengaban had treated her.

"Go gather yer things, then," the captain said, turning away.

Elbriarien nodded, understanding the captain's need to leave instead of staying and chatting for a good while. The captain had a whole ship to look after. She could take care of herself.

It didn't take her long to pack up her single backpack which she strapped easily to her back. It had been a parting gift from her parents, grudgingly given to show at least some support for her new venture. It was made from the black, supple leather of tanned polar bear hides, then it had been well-oiled and treated to keep all weather out. It wasn't magically enchanted, but it was so well made, it might well have been magical.

Elbriarien walked back up to the upper deck and quickly said her goodbyes. The rest of the crew was busy with the cargo so no one really had time for her. She did promise to come back in a week's time to see them off.

Then Elbriarien straightened her back, set her gaze for the city, forced herself to walk down the plank, off the ship, her sanctuary, and into the crowds.

CHAPTER THREE

Elbriarien stood on the street outside of what she presumed was *The Book Ends* inn. The carved wooden sign showed three books with numbers on their spines. On either side of the books, a pair of carved book ends stood. The numbers on the books were out of order: 2, 10, and 4. She didn't understand the significance of them.

She'd found the inn as promised, up on the third tier of Osirholm as counted rising from the harbor. She could no longer see the piers, just a line of water out across the horizon. The air was hotter up here without the salty ocean breezes. Drier as well. Yet, the neighborhood still seemed rich to her, with plenty of trees and beautiful gardens tucked in between pastel-colored houses and businesses. The houses here were mostly built out of thick walls of stone, to keep them insulated against the heat. However, all the roofs were flat. No one needed steeply peaked coverings to shed snow, or possibly even that much rain.

After taking yet another deep breath, Elbriarien pushed open the door of the inn, stepping into the cool darkness.

She paused for a moment on the threshold, blinking to clear her vision, letting it adjust from the bright mid-morning sunlight to the dimmer interior.

To the left, along the entire length of the room, ran a bar. Behind it, two huge kegs hung from the ceiling on thick iron chains. Three shelves lined the wall behind them, filled with both clay pots and glass bottles, probably holding different types of liquor for creating drinks.

"We're closed," came a voice out of a dark corner just beyond the bar. "Come back at dinner."

"Uhm, Captain Masym sent me? Told me to ask for Nellie?" Elbriarien said, uncertain.

"What are you looking for?" The voice seemed melodious to Elbriarien, with a lilting quality that made her think the person was used to singing. At least the person seemed curious, and not hostile. The tone was mid-range, so El couldn't guess as to the gender of the speaker.

"A room," El said. "And employment."

"Really? An ice maiden? Here?" the voice mused.

A shadow moved.

No, it was an Umber Elf.

El couldn't help but stare. She'd never seen one of their kind before.

The other Elf stood as tall as El, thin and graceful, with pointed ears and sharp features.

That was where their likenesses ended.

While El's skin was as white as freshly fallen snow, and her hair was long and chestnut-brown, the Umber Elf had skin so black the Elf blended into the shadows even without magic. Red eyes peered at El, like two coals burning in the dark. Her hair was as white as an elder's, though El didn't believe the other person was that old. It spiked all around her head, like a mane. She wore a plain tan sleeveless tunic that hung down over gray pants that ended at the knee. Gold rings pierced the entire outer edge of her right ear, and a glittering blue gem at least two inches across hung around her neck.

"Yes, I am an Ice Elf," El said, feeling a little defensive.

"You can get all the work you'd like, then," the other Elf said. "Everyone will be looking for ice from you."

El sighed and held up her left arm, showing her clear skin. "I have no mark. I cannot work as an Ice Mage."

"But you know spells for ice, right?" the Elf said. "You can make it as cold as ye want."

"True," El said slowly. "But it's against the King's Law for me to practice without a Mage Mark."

"Eh, true enough," the Umber Elf said. She held up her arm, where two silver bands glowed against her dark skin. "I do desert magic, for all the good it does here, in the city," she added. "And I'm Nel. Neladrie Kealgor. I run this establishment with my husband, Kucher."

"I'm El—Elbriarien Itamar—newly arrived here and looking for some way—some legal way—to support myself," El said. "I have a bit of money, so I can live for a while before I find something. Eventually, though, I'll need to work."

A door banged open at the back of a bar, and a short Human male came bustling through. "Nel! The latest shipment of booze just came in from the north. You won't believe what I managed to pick up!"

He pulled to a stop when he saw that Nel wasn't alone. He looked like Captain Masym to El's untutored eye—short, squat, and muscular, though he had fiery orange hair and a bushy mustache that took over his entire top lip. He wore overalls, with just a bib on top and no shirt underneath.

"Hello there!" he said, in a very friendly fashion. "We're not open yet," he added, still with a huge smile on his face.

"She knows, Kucher," Nel said dryly. "She's looking for work."

The Human gave El a speculative look. "We have that Dwarvish ice machine, so we don't really need help at the bar," he said.

El blinked in surprise. She'd never thought about what type of work she'd be doing, though she knew that without her Mage Mark, she couldn't do magical things.

"Can't. Not an Ice Mage," Nel said.

"Ah. Then we can't help her, I'm afraid," Kucher said, his smile turning apologetic.

"We can help her get settled," Nel said, stepping forward. "She needs a room. And some contacts."

"We can help with those," Kucher said, his smile brightening again.

El had the feeling that not much ever deterred the man.

Nel quickly negotiated a price for the room for a week. It cost much less than El had been expecting. Either the prices in the north were really high, or Nel felt sorry for her and was giving her a good deal.

The room was simple but impeccably clean, with a washbasin next to the door, a bed that was narrow but long enough for an Elf, and a plain wooden wardrobe for hanging clothes. Colorful yellow and blue tile covered the walls, forming flowers in a mosaic design, while the floor was all a dark red tile. It felt both homey as well as fresh.

Once El had unpacked a few belongings and settled in, she went back downstairs, determined to do some exploring of the city. Nel and Kucher were standing on either side of the bar with their heads together, talking quietly.

"I know you said that you could wait a while before you started your employment, but would you mind interviewing for something now? It's just come up, and I think you'd be perfect for it!" Kucher said enthusiastically.

El glanced over at Nel, who shrugged. While she wasn't as enthusiastic as her husband, she didn't appear to think it was a bad idea.

"Sure," El said.

"Great! Let's go!" Kucher said. He went up onto his toes to kiss his wife tenderly on her cheek before heading back out the front door.

"You don't have to take it, if they offer it to you," Nel said quietly as El was about to step outside. "But I think it'll be good for ye."

"All right," El said as she stepped back outside into the light and heat of the day.

It was even more crowded now than it had been earlier. However, the enthusiasm of Kucher, and the way he deftly wove his way through the people, gave El confidence.

She could do this.

Even if she wasn't quite certain what "this" was.

CHAPTER FOUR

Kucher gave lively commentary as they walked, pointing out restaurants that El would want to try, the market she should walk through, the best herbalist in town, and so on.

It filled her with joy that he thought so much of the city and its merchants. Everyone appeared to be his friend, as he waved and nodded at people. No one approached, though they did give long looks at El, maybe trying to identify what type of being she was.

"You must know everyone in Osirholm," she commented as they rounded the curve at the end of the street and started heading up to the next tier.

"Eh, only about half," Kucher said.

"Which half?" El teased as he waved at two men walking beside their horses as they navigated an overfilled cart down the street.

"The half worth knowing, of course," Kucher said with a wink.

After they reached the fourth tier, he led them off the main thoroughfare, into a quieter street. The houses here were even bigger than El had been expecting: mansions with huge yards and brilliant flowers in the gardens.

Kucher followed the road around and led her to one of the smaller houses that was tucked in between a couple of larger ones. It only had two stories (as opposed to the three plus rooftop courtyard of its neighbors) and lovely mauve walls. The flat roof reflected the sunlight, and pretty flowers filled the yard. She heard the shrieks of children playing from somewhere inside.

"Now, Gyles Margravine and his wife, Ceceline, are looking for someone to live with them for the summer and to look after their two children, Sigder and Wyne," Kucher explained. "In addition to room and board, you'll have a bit of pocket change. It isn't much, and the job is only for a few months. But it will give you the opportunity to look around, see what else you might want to do. A holding place, as it were."

El blinked, surprised. It actually sounded perfect. Though she'd never had a sister or brother, she did have younger cousins whom she'd dealt with when she'd still been living at home, frequently babysitting the youngsters while the adults gathered to work (and gossip).

"Let's go see them," El said, indicating that Kucher should lead the way down the charming stone pathway.

"Eh, I think it would be better for you to go knocking on the door yourself," Kucher said. For the first time that morning, he seemed uncomfortable. "See, they only know me as a bar-owner. Not the kind of person they want to associate with. Whereas you, well, you're you."

El had no idea what he meant by that. "I don't understand."

"You're beautiful. Elvish. Exotic. Educated. Magical. The

Margravines couldn't hire anyone better, not even if they paid three times what they're offering," Kucher said.

He'd already told her a few more details about the job and the coin they'd pay. Now, he patiently waited for her to open the gate to the garden.

"I'll be just down the street," he promised. "At *The Broken Blade.* I won't abandon you."

El watched him walk away with a jaunty step, then turned to face the house again.

It still seemed cheery. Inviting, even. Unfamiliar flowers filled the garden, and she longed to know the name and the various properties of every single one. The neighborhood was so much quieter than the busy main streets. It would be a good place for her to find her feet.

She'd faced down ice demons and certain doom. She could certainly talk to a couple of Humans about a job.

Pulling up her courage, El straightened her shoulders and walked through the gate, toward the house.

Before she reached the door, it suddenly flew open and a young boy, maybe ten years old, came racing out. On his heels was a younger girl, maybe eight. They both had blond-brown hair, tanned skin, and freckles. They were the kind of scrawny that active children had, when they were growing so fast it was almost impossible to keep meat on their bones. They each had on a simple short-sleeved shirt, shorts, and sandals, all done in tones of green and brown.

And neither of them were looking where they were going.

Instead of letting the boy in front plow into her, El stepped to the side, but held out a hand to catch his arm as he went by.

"What, what?" the boy said, looking up at El in alarm.

The girl came pelting up. El had to put out a hand to stop her from running down the boy, pressing her palm firmly into the girl's chest.

"Give me back my book!" the girl yelled, heedless of who was holding her back.

"I don't have your stupid book," the boy said. "Don't you remember? You lost it by the gazebo out back weeks ago."

"I did not," the girl said stubbornly. "I was reading it just this morning. And now it's gone."

"I didn't take it," the boy said.

El could tell he was lying. She still had a hand on his arm and the way he'd tensed told her something wasn't right.

"If you didn't take it, where did it go?" El asked him, still not letting go of his arm.

"I don't know," he said sullenly, still tense but not because some unknown adult was questioning him.

"Could it be in your room?" El mused. "Or in the kitchen perhaps? In the garden? Maybe the front sitting room, where your parents greet guests?"

"We're not supposed to go there," the girl said, suddenly wary, as if just realizing that this was a stranger.

However, the way that the boy stiffened up further told El exactly where he'd hidden his sister's book.

"I need to go talk with your parents," El said as she released the boy's arm and moved her hand away from in front of the girl. "If you would like to go with me, perhaps we can find your book."

The boy suddenly looked worried. "Maybe someone else took your book. Moved it. You know how Brytha gets when she's in a cleaning tizzy."

The girl gave a snort of derision. She knew what was up.

"Tell me the name of your book, and I'll see if I can find it while I speak with your parents," El said. She didn't want to get the boy into trouble. That wouldn't be a good way to start their relationship. But he shouldn't have taken the girl's book, either.

"*Corbray's Illustrated Guide to Herbs of Annund*," the girl announced triumphantly.

"Really?" El gave her a look. Though El wasn't great at judging the age of Humans, she knew the girl wasn't that old. Was she actually reading such a weighty tome?

The girl nodded firmly, then added more shyly, "I like the pictures."

The boy snorted at that, and would have made a snarky comment but looked warily at El and changed his mind.

"All right," El said. "I will see you both out here after I'm finished," she said.

The pair of siblings nodded and El walked up to the house.

The door was already open, so she just poked her head inside. "Hello?" she called out.

A very short being bustled down the hallway. "Aye, miss. What can I do for ye?"

It took El a few moments to realize that the person she faced was, in fact, a Dwarf. She was taller than most of the Dwarves who El had met, coming almost up to her chest. However, she had the same solid build as the rest of them, with long black hair that had been done into braids that she wore up on her head like a crown. She had on a heavily embroidered white shirt under a black vest, with a long black skirt.

"I'm here to apply for the position? To look after the

children?" El said, indicating the pair of siblings still standing in the yard, whispering urgently at each other.

"Aye, that's good. The young'uns need looking after, what with their parents so busy and all," the Dwarf said. "I'm Brytha, and I tend to all the things in the household. You ever need a thing, you come to me."

"Thank you, Brytha, I'm El. Elbriarien Itamar. Pleased to make your acquaintance."

Brytha gave her a broad grin. "Let me be checking with Master Margravine, see if he can speak with ye now. Lady Ceceline is out at the moment."

El nodded and Brytha bustled away, tapping at a door to the right of the entranceway.

The front hallway was elegant, even for a Human household, full of heavy wood and tile floors. A grand staircase started in the middle of the space, leading up to the second floor. Closed doors hid rooms on either side, all the way to the back of the mansion.

Brytha returned in just a few moments. "Come, sit, and the master will be right with ye. Can I get ye something to drink? Water? Tea?"

"Some water would be lovely, thank you," El said as she followed Brytha into a room to the left of the door, opposite the first one Brytha had gone into.

The front sitting room had the same rich feeling as the hallway, with heavy wooden furniture that was black and glossy, dark red pillows, and gold curtains draped over the windows.

There, on the end table of the formal couch, sat a book with the title of *Corbray's Illustrated Guide to Herbs of Annund*. It looked old and well-loved, the green cloth cover frayed at the edges. A beautiful illustration of a lady slipper, a plant that El recognized from the north, decorated the front of it.

She picked up the book and flipped through the pages. The girl was right, it did have some lovely pictures in it. El sat down on the couch and continued glancing through the pages when Brytha came back in.

"Here ye go, dear," she said, carrying a tray that had two tall glasses along with a crystal pitcher filled with pure water.

"Thank you, Brytha," came a deep voice from the open doorway. "That will be all."

El put the book down on the couch and rose to greet Gyles Margravine. He was tall for a Human, not quite able to look her in the eye but close. He wore a white shirt with a starched collar, closed at the neck with a light blue tie bound in an elegant knot. A dove-gray vest with matching trousers and shiny black shoes completed his look.

He appeared to be in his mid-forties. His blond-brown hair had threads of white running through it, and his tanned face had wrinkles around his eyes and mouth.

El placed one hand over the other, then rested both on the front of her chest before bowing her head in greeting.

When she looked up, she saw that Gyles had a strange expression on his face—as though he were confused—before he gave her the same greeting in return.

It was only then that El remembered that people down here sometimes shook hands, or even grasped forearms, as a way of greeting one another.

Oh well.

"I am Elbriarien Itamar," she said as Gyles straightened back up. "I heard that you have need of a tutor, for the children."

"We do," Gyles said as he seated himself, pouring her a

glass of water then one for himself. "We just put out word yesterday afternoon, so I'm surprised that anyone is responding so quickly," he explained. "The children's regular tutor has taken a leave of absence, to go and visit his family for the summer. Then, his replacement met with a serious accident, and so we are abruptly without someone. Tell me, what are your qualifications?"

"I don't have any children of my own, of course," El said. Though she knew Elves who'd had their children early, most waited at least until their second century. "But I did care for my younger cousins anytime the family gathered together."

"Did you give them any lessons?" Gyles asked.

"Like reading, maths, and the sort?" El said. At his nod, she continued. "Yes. I helped Amarien learn her letters, and I frequently did sums with Alios. We sang the old songs together, and I taught them the history of the Ice Elves."

"In Elvish?"

"Yes, High Elvish. I also speak Dwarvish fluently. And while I have a solid base of Gnomish, I'm not fluent." The Ice Elves, like the Umber and Wood Elves, all had their own dialects. High Elvish was understood by all Elves. While local Dwarves and Gnomes had their own idioms and colloquiums, they all had a common tongue. In addition, everyone spoke Common, though some not as well as others.

"Good, good," Gyles said. "Now, don't take this the wrong way, but what sort of magic do you practice?"

El frowned, puzzled by the question, but she still answered. "I have my own Ice Elf magic that I use. Cantrips, and such," El said. She held up her left wrist, showing her unmarked skin. "But I'm not an Ice Mage, if that's what you're asking about. I cannot do spoken spells. Not without breaking the King's Law."

"Excellent!" Gyles said. "The children are of an age where they need to buckle down. To stop being so extravagant about things. When they start putting aside the things of childhood for the things of adulthood. Having a tutor who is always casting magic is going to give them the wrong idea."

"Are you against magic?" El said, still confused.

"No, no, not at all," Gyles tried to reassure her. "It's just that there really isn't any magical ability in our family. The children, no matter how hard they try, are never going to be able to do spells on their own. But they're also fascinated by it, and have dreams that they might be able to."

El had known that some Humans had less magical abilities than the others. Wizards tended to come from particular families. Rarely did someone from outside that direct lineage have a lot of magic.

However, she'd also believed that anyone could cast magic if they worked hard enough at it. Sure, they might not have the talent or strength of others, but they could still do some things.

Right?

"I won't be doing extravagant spells in front of the children, if that's what you're afraid of," El said. "I won't break the King's Law."

"Good, good," Gyles said, seeming to relax. "So tell me more about yourself."

El decided to not tell him of her failed apprenticeship. Instead, she talked about always longing to go see the world, to travel on her own, to experience constant summer for a while. Of the tales that the Bard Gytha had told her, and how that had colored her experiences.

Gyles seemed pleased by her tale and offered her the position immediately. Though he didn't state so explicitly, she got the impression that what Kucher had said was true: the Margravines couldn't have asked for a better person for their tutor. They negotiated a bit—El managed to get a higher rate than he'd originally offered, plus not moving in until the next day, giving her the evening to spend at *The Book Ends* inn.

As she stood to go, she picked up the book that had been seated innocently on the couch beside her. "I have a great interest in the flora of the world," she said. "May I borrow this?"

"Of course, of course," Gyles said. "In fact, that might become one of your teaching books."

El managed not to roll her eyes at that. While there were fantastic illustrations in the book, the text was exceedingly dry.

Still, maybe she could take the children on walks, and the three of them could learn to identify all the flowers in the nearby gardens...

"Thank you," El said. "I will see you about this time tomorrow morning."

"Until then," Gyles said. "If you need anything, just ask Brytha."

El soon found herself outside the house, book and job in hand.

She hadn't taken two steps before the two youngsters came running up to her.

"You found it!" the girl exclaimed.

"I did. Someone had placed it in the front sitting room," she said, giving a knowing look at the boy. "Your father suggested that I use it as one of your teaching texts."

"Oh," the girl said, suddenly wary.

"Are you to be our summer tutor?" the boy asked.

"I am. My name is Elbriarien Itamar, but you can call me El," she said.

"I'm Wyne," the girl said. "And this one is Sigder, my brother."

"Very pleased to make your acquaintance," El said, nodding her head at first one, then the other.

"Can you do magic?" Sigder asked.

El smiled, glad she'd been forewarned. "A little," she said. "Just the things that are natural to an Ice Elf. Cantrips, but not spells."

"Can't you, like, create huge ice storms or something?" Sigder said.

"Even if I could, I can't do any spells here," El said, once again lifting her left arm. "I have no Mage Mark. And I won't break the King's Law."

They both nodded solemnly at that, though El could tell that Sigder wasn't about to drop the topic for good.

"I am to start as your tutor tomorrow," El added as the siblings continued to look at her, speculating. "I'm sure we'll learn all about each other over the summer."

"But not too many lessons, right?" Sigder said.

"I don't know. Surely a smart boy like you would like extra lessons?" El teased.

Both El and Wyne giggled at his sour expression.

"I'll try to make the lessons as interesting as I can," El promised.

Before they could pelt her with any more questions, El said her goodbyes and walked through the far gate.

She had a job. A place to stay for the summer.

Everything was turning out just fine.

CHAPTER FIVE

El found Kucher at *The Broken Blade*, a stuffy tavern that had glass (glass!) tables, iron chairs, and blinding white walls.

No brawl would dare raise its head in here.

On the way back to *The Book Ends*, Kucher took her down a staircase to get from one tier to the next instead of along the road.

"Going down always feels easier on me thighs then going up," he grumbled as he took the stairs one at a time.

El nodded in sympathy. The stairs were spaced such that she could easily go from one step to the next, but someone as short as Kucher might have difficulty.

"Are there other, easier staircases?" El had to ask. Only Humans appeared to use this one. Surely there were ones better suited to the Dwarves and Gnomes, which Kucher might use, given his lack of height.

"There are, but they're too far out of our way," Kucher grumbled.

The staircase dropped them off at a small local market, which Kucher gladly led her through, claiming to help her get a feel for the place. While that may have been part of the reason, they also spent a good deal of time chatting first with one vendor then another, as Kucher appeared to know everyone there as well. He introduced her to all the merchants, though she wasn't sure how much shopping she'd be doing, as her new tutoring job gave her not only room but board as well.

They returned to the inn by mid-afternoon. El was grateful for the excuse to go to her room and lie down for a bit. The bed supported her comfortably and she found herself dozing though the heat of the afternoon. The tile decorating her walls and floor made so much more sense now, as it held onto the coolness of the night before.

By the time El opened her eyes again, the sun was almost at the horizon. The buildings standing to the west cast long shadows. She judged it to be less than an hour to sunset. The city was just starting to wake up.

El made her way down to the tavern room. Only three tables had people sitting at them. The one that caught her eye had a pair of Dwarves with several glasses already scattered across their table, trying what looked like a large collection of different drinks.

"Nel! A little more of the *Krumbka* liquor, and splash in some pomegranate this time!" one of them called.

Nel rolled her eyes at El but did as her guest asked, pouring a shiny yellow liqueur out of a tall glass bottle into two glasses, then adding in some dark red syrup.

She brought the drinks over to the Dwarves, then sidled up to where El stood at the bar. "Yer room doesn't include dinner, but I'm happy to serve ye some wine on the house."

"I was just about to ask where I should go get some

food," El said. "Kucher took me to a market, which was lovely, but I don't really know how to cook."

That got her a sympathetic snort. "I hear ye. Somehow, my skills at roasting scorpions and desert rats over an open fire aren't in high demand in the city."

"Imagine that," El said dryly. "The sailors on the boat I came in on didn't care for pickled seaweed, either."

"No accounting for taste," Nel said with a shake of her head and a sly grin. "If ye go east down the main street, past three more streets, ye'll hear the night market before ye get there. There'll be plenty to choose from there."

"Raw fish?" El asked, slightly hopeful.

"Probably not," Nel admitted. "Though more than one stall will sell you fried crickets."

El opened her mouth then closed it again. That didn't sound appetizing at all. Then again, she'd been told the seaweed she'd tried to serve the crew hadn't worked for them, despite how carefully she'd pickled it.

"I'll see what I can find," El assured her.

El stepped out into the surprisingly busy main street. Most of the towns she'd visited on her way down the coast had all started to slow down as dusk approached. Not Osirholm. Maybe it was because people rested during the heat of the day.

Though Humans made up the majority of the people El saw, most of the other races were represented as well. She didn't see another Ice Elf, but she did see more than one Wood Elf, as well as a couple of Umber Elves. Dwarves probably made up the next largest part of the population, followed by Gnomes. El didn't see a being she didn't recognize, though some did make her smile, particularly the group of young Gnomes with riotous-colored hair, along with just as bold stripes of paint streaking their faces.

As Nel predicted, El heard the market long before she got there. Smelled it, too. Though El still missed the food from her childhood, she had quickly gotten accustomed to cooked meat and even grilled fish.

The night market had taken over what El suspected was a regular market during the day: a long covered rectangle that went on for four blocks, stuffed with stalls of vendors.

The scent of chicken cooking over a fire drew her in first, making her mouth water. Wooden skewers held small pieces of chicken, interspersed with bits of red onion, shriveled mushrooms, and small red fruit that she'd learned were called tomatoes. A heady mixture of herbs had been sprinkled on top of the skewers, adding to the delicious smell.

After purchasing two, and subsequently burning both her fingers and her tongue, El started walking through the night market. Even though the sun had yet to fully set, magical lights glowed on sticks set at regular intervals, making it as bright as day under the overhead covering.

The markets El had visited earlier with Kucher had seemed more sedate, with people just going about their business. The night market, on the other hand, had more of a sense of playfulness, as though a party was about to burst out at the stall just ahead. Or perhaps someone would bring out a flute and there would be dancing.

Probably not the sedate dancing that Elves did, but maybe the whirling tops that Gnomes emulated, or even the foot stomping of Dwarves.

Everything El could imagine was for sale here, as well as several things she didn't think she'd ever need, such as hair dyes and face paint, the kinds that the Gnomes favored. She'd never seen such cleverly woven baskets and bags, the straw dyed and then woven brilliantly. One stand had lovely capes for keeping off the heat of the sun as well as the coolness of the evening. Another had hats that would do an adequate job, something she might want to purchase later, depending on her charges and how their days went.

El wandered from one end of the market to the other, then back again. She debated buying another chicken skewer, but decided instead to try some other delicacy.

The Ice Elves didn't bake much, except for holidays and festivals. Outside of their lands, El had seen a lot more baked goods, from piles of flat bread to glazed and sweetened rolls.

El started to make her way toward one of the vendors who was selling what looked like sticks of something baked and then rolled in sugar when a flash of magic stopped her cold.

Throughout the day, she hadn't seen *anyone* casting magic, nothing flashy at any rate. Some people did have a magical glow to them—El knew she did, given that she constantly cooled herself as well as protecting her skin from the sun. She assumed other people did similar things.

She walked toward where she'd seen the flash. She didn't start to hurry until she realized that no one else had seen the casting.

Was she the only magical being in the vicinity who'd been trained to see spells? She'd learned how as part of her apprenticeship, to be able to judge the strength of a demon, as well as how much magic her fellow Elves had remaining during a prolonged battle.

The Human woman standing behind the counter selling rolls covered in sugar and glazed with icing had a dazed look in her eyes, while the Human man in front of her was grabbing as many rolls as he could and stuffing them in a bag. The vendors on either side of her didn't seem to be noticing anything either.

"Hey! What are you doing?" El asked as she came up.

The man froze and glanced over his shoulder at her.

"Nothing!" he squeaked.

Though El wasn't great at judging the ages of anyone, she knew that this person was young. Perhaps in his twenties.

Much too young to be a Master and casting spells.

She grabbed his left forearm—the one holding the bag—and lifted it so she could see his wrist, to see if he had a Mage Mark.

He appeared to recognize what she wanted and pushed her away with his other hand before she got a good look. Another flash of magic momentarily blinded El and she found herself tumbling to the ground.

Generally, El would never have fallen. Elves were usually too graceful. However, this man (boy?) wore an amulet around his neck that appeared to greatly enhance his native power. It had flared as he'd pushed her.

El shook her head and sprang to her feet, ready to do battle.

The boy was gone. Had he cast yet another spell and turned invisible? Was that why she could no longer see him in the crowd?

A groan from the woman in the stall drew El's attention.

El realized she held the bag of pilfered rolls in her hand. She must have grabbed it when the boy had pushed her. She put it on the table with the other goods and hurried around, coming to stand in front of the other woman.

"Are you all right?" El asked.

The Human's head maybe came up to El's collarbone.

Her short brown hair stood out all around her head in kinky curls. Brown eyes blinked in confusion and she swayed. Her skin was brown as well, as if she'd spent her life out in the sunlight, though El suspected that brown was just the woman's natural color.

El reached out and wrapped her hand around the woman's bicep, holding the woman steady as she started to sway. The tan cloth of the seller's blouse felt surprisingly smooth, much more so than El had been expecting. The merchant must make good money selling her rolls.

El put her other hand up to the woman's forehead. Foreign, unexpected magic sometimes burned a body, at least among the Ice Elves. However, the Human woman didn't appear overly warm. El brought her hand down and snapped her fingers in front of the woman's eyes.

That brought the woman back to the present.

"What—what happened?" she said, glancing at El before immediately looking at her table. "Oh no!"

El pointed at the bag with all the rolls. "There was a Human male here. With magic. He'd cast a spell to stop you from noticing him while he robbed you."

"You saw him?" the woman asked, her gaze suddenly focused.

"I did," El said. "He was young. Maybe still a boy. With an amulet around his neck that flared when he cast magic." She grimaced. "I don't think he's a Master, just some fool who's gotten in over his head."

How had he acquired that amulet? And made it work? Where was his Master? Did he have one? Mages regularly created small magical items, or temporarily imbued items with magic, like the Ice Mages and their spears. However, those sorts of artifacts had a single purpose. El had never heard of, or even seen, an amulet that enhanced one's power overall.

"I'm Frysa," the woman said as she reached for the bag. She opened it, then frowned. "I'm not sure I can sell these." She looked up at El. "There have been quite a few thefts this past month in the market. Merchants who, though they claimed to be standing behind their stall the entire time, suddenly found half their goods gone."

"Mainly food?" El said.

Frysa nodded, still picking through the bag, pulling out the rolls that were the least crushed. "Aye. Maybe a few other items have gone missing, like a cloak or a bag, but those might just be common theft."

"A bag like the one you're holding?" El said pointedly.

Frysa gasped. "Yes," she said slowly, drawing out the sound. "I do think Myree is missing something like this." She held it up to El, who now could see the fine weaving and the subtle pattern of chevrons done in various shades of black and tan.

"You need to set some guards who can see magic to watch over the market," El said. "He wasn't very subtle about the spells he cast."

"You can see magic being cast?" Frysa said, peering at El.

"I can." Then El made the oh-too-familiar motion of holding up her left arm, to show her bare wrist. "But I can't be hired. I'm not a Mage."

Frysa nodded, understanding. "I'll bring it up with the Merchants' Guild. Let them know what's going on. They'll find someone to watch the market."

She glanced down at the bag of rolls, then back at El. "Here," she said. "I can't sell the rest of these. Take these as a thank you for stopping the theft."

"You don't need to pay me for doing the right thing," El said slowly.

Frysa smiled for the first time. "I know. But you did the right thing. And that should be rewarded."

El opened her mouth then closed it again. Frysa's gesture was something that all of the Ice Elves she knew would do. As well as most of the crew from *The Piebald Pup.*

"I'm new here," El said as she walked out from behind the table, to stand on the other side. "I'm not sure where I could take these."

"Where are you staying?" Frysa said.

"At *The Book Ends*," El said.

"Take them to Kucher. He'll have use for them," Frysa assured her. "He's good at taking advantage of any windfall," she added dryly.

El wasn't surprised that Frysa knew Kucher. She was glad that the baker was one of the half of the people the innkeeper thought was worth knowing.

"I'll give them to him," El said with a grin. She glanced around the market, but she didn't see the boy anywhere. "And I'll keep my eye out for the boy."

"Aye, do that. Can I send someone from the guild to visit with you? To get more of a description?" Frysa said.

"Of course, though I won't be at the inn after tomorrow." El gave her the address of the Margravines, explaining her new position.

"Well, if you can bring the children here some night, I'll make sure they have a delightful treat," Frysa promised.

"That isn't necessary," El said. She could pay for what the children had.

Or perhaps ask Brytha for some pocket change.

"It is," Frysa said earnestly. "If nothing else, as an additional thank you. We need to catch this false Mage. Before he does more harm. At least we finally have a clue about who's responsible for these thefts. So thank you, again, for stopping him."

"You're welcome," El said, though she still didn't feel as though she'd done much of anything.

She nibbled on one of the rolls as she walked back out of the market. The bread was soft, yet flaky at the same time. She couldn't identify the spices mixed in, as they were all foreign to her. It was sweet, warming, and spicy, all at the same time.

El would have to remember this night market, and come back to visit Frysa sometime. To find out if the Merchants' Guild had found the boy.

And also to have another of these delicious rolls.

CHAPTER SIX

Despite staying up late the night before, as well as having a glass of something called brandy that went amazingly well with one of the rolls that Frysa had sent, El found herself awake early the next morning.

Though the sun was up, El felt as though the city still dozed around her. Maybe it, too, had been up too late the night before.

El washed her face in the clean water in the washbasin, took care of her morning needs, then walked out of the inn, into the coolness of the morning.

A small market with only a few stalls had already been set up in the space occupied by the night market. El still had a roll from Frysa, and bought herself a cup of tea from one of the busier stands.

The tea had dark, bitter notes that El found she enjoyed, mixed in with some type of mint. Mostly she had drunk herbal teas up north, but she'd grown to like the teas popular among the Humans. They gave her a lot more energy. Sometimes too much, and she'd end up shaking.

El walked slowly down to the harbor as the city woke up around her. Captain Masym was awake and welcomed her back aboard *The Piebald Pup*.

Captain Masym shook his shaggy head after she told him about her new job. "Can't say I'm surprised ye got yerself settled so fast," he said. "Don't know the Margravines meself, but they got themselves a bargain, they did. So ye'll only be seeing after the children? No housekeeping?"

"I don't think so," El said. "They have a housekeeper, a Dwarf named Brytha."

"That's good, that's good," Captain Masym said. "The crew'll miss yer winds. But maybe not yer cooking."

El snorted. "I'll have to learn to make something you'll enjoy, to surprise you with the next time you're in port."

Captain Masym grinned. "As long as I don't have to lie and tell ye I like it."

"What, not even to save my feelings?" El said in mock hurt.

"Pshaw. Rather hurt them than scorch me tastebuds," he replied.

El managed not to roll her eyes. "You just wait," she said.

Though after El left the boat, she wasn't certain. She wouldn't be cooking, not at the Margravines. Brytha—or some other servant—would be doing that. All she could do would be to educate her own tastebuds, to learn about the various herbs and flavors preferred down here. It would mean a lot of going out and trying new foods at the various markets.

Darn.

Back at the inn, it didn't take El long to pack up—she'd barely gotten unpacked. Nel stood behind the bar when El went back downstairs, ready to leave.

"Here you go," Nel said, handing El back all of her coins.

"But I owe you for one night," El said, unwilling to live on charity.

"And then you brought all those rolls in," Nel said. "You might not have realized that Kucher was selling them off in the corner. We made a profit off those, even subtracting the cost of your room."

"You did give me a free glass of brandy for that," El said, still not moving to pick up the coins from the bar.

"Still running in the black," Nel insisted. "Plus, you came here because Captain Masym told you to. You'll tell someone else. I'll make it up."

"Are you sure?" El asked.

"I'm sure," Nel said. "Besides, you need enough to buy some of those fried crickets at the market."

El rolled her eyes as she picked up her coins. "Have you ever tried them?"

"Nope," Nel said with a grin. "Never been that desperate. Supposedly they come in more than one flavor. I've heard the red ones—the spicy ones—are the best."

El shuddered. She didn't want to say that she only ate bland food, but that might not be too far from the truth. Spicy food didn't necessarily agree with her, as she'd never had it growing up.

"I'll keep that in mind," she promised. Or at least she'd remember to never eat the red fried crickets, if she did go ahead and try them someday.

After saying goodbye, and promising to come and visit soon, El slowly made her way up to the next highest tier in the city, up to the Margravines, taking the long way up the road instead of trying a staircase. She had no trouble remembering the way. She found it so much easier to find landmarks in a city, where markers that were easy to remember were strewn along the way. In the frozen tundra, every snow-covered lump and valley looked the same, and even an Ice Elf could get lost. Here, she had merchant shops, colorful houses, and even the occasional street name to navigate by.

Brytha opened the door when El knocked. "Good to see ye, miss," Brytha said as she indicated that El should follow her. "Is that all ye have?" she asked curiously, looking at the solid black-leather pack El carried.

"Yes," El said. "I've been traveling, and haven't really acquired much."

"We'll have to take care of that, then," Brytha said with a determined nod of her head. "Ye need to go to the market, give me a holler. I'll go with ye, and get ye the best price."

El didn't bother to hide her grin, remembering the bargaining prowess of the Dwarves on the ship. "I will. Thank you."

The room Brytha led her to was up on the second floor, at the back of the house. Bright white paint covered the brick walls, while a rougher stone made up the floor. It would be cool in the summer, and cooler in the winter. Fortunately, El didn't mind the cold.

Unbleached sheets and a fuzzy blue blanket that covered the bed stretched underneath the two windows that overlooked the back garden. Bright morning sunshine spilled across the bed and onto the floor, giving the place a kind of charm. In the corner to the right stood a series of shelves with a plain curtain to draw over them, the equivalent of a wardrobe. The washbasin rested next to the door, and held a pretty blue-and-white ceramic bowl for washing, along with a matching pitcher.

"Oh, I'll have Henry bring in a chair for ye," Brytha said, looking around as El placed her bag on the bed.

"Thank you," El said. She knew there was a room set up as a classroom, so she wouldn't have to be teaching the children in her bedroom.

She'd like a rug, and maybe some decorations for the wall, to make the room less austere. That meant trips to the market, with something in mind to buy, which would be fun.

Brytha led El back downstairs, showing her the back staircase that wasn't anywhere near as grand as the front one. El understood that she should use this staircase from now on. She wasn't quite a servant, but she was no longer a valued guest, either.

The kitchen was larger than El's room. A good sized, magical cast-iron stove took up most of one wall. A sink with a small pump that brought water inside sat along another wall. Beside it stood a Dwarvish ice box that El could sense a small trickle of magic flowing through. A large set of shelves covered the last wall, holding plates, cups, bowls, silverware, and serving dishes, enough to provide a meal for over a dozen people. More shelves and a door opening out onto the back gardens filled the last wall. In the center of the kitchen, a huge table used for preparing food took up most of the rest of the space.

Brytha introduced El to Vorwin, the Gnome cook, who stood on a wooden box in order to reach the top of the stove. Though El hadn't met many Gnomes, Vorwin struck her as more pudgy than the few she'd known, with ample folds of orangish skin around her face and neck, broad arms, very large breasts, and a rotund belly. Round, amber-colored eyes stared at El with glee. Vorwin wore an outfit similar to

Brytha's—white shirt, black vest, but with black pants that ended just below her knees instead of a long skirt. While Vorwin's shirt didn't have the heavy embroidery that Brytha's did, her hair more than made up for it, as pink, blue, and pale green streaks adorned her wild spikes.

"Have you eaten yet?" Vorwin asked, looking El up and down. "I've got lots to help fatten you up."

"Uhm, no, thank you. I had something already," El said, a little uncertain.

Brytha rolled her eyes. "Not everyone needs to be up to yer standards of weight," she said.

Vorwin shrugged. "Skinny girl like you isn't going to catch a mate," she warned El, pointing at her with the spoon she'd been using to stir her pot. "Need to be hefty. Weighty. Show that you're wealthy enough to take care of him."

"I see," El said. "Maybe that's been my problem all these years." That, and always fighting on edges of the frozen wastelands. Sure, she'd had the occasional lover, but she'd never found anyone she'd wanted to share her life with. Either female or male.

"Eh, you look healthy enough," Vorwin said magnanimously. "But I'll get some meat on your bones. Don't you worry."

"Thank you?" El said, unsure of what else to say.

"Anything you really like to eat? Dislike?" Vorwin asked, peering closely at El.

"We always ate raw fish at home," El said. "And mushrooms. And pickled lake greens."

Vorwin gave a visible shudder. "Surprised you reached that height with that kind of grub."

"My parents did their best," El said dryly.

"S'alright. You're here now. In the kitchen of Vorwin Squigglecase. I'll take care of you. Ye just watch."

El smiled. "I'm not used to spicy food," she added, figuring that she should warn Vorwin.

That just got her a nod. "Yup. Beige. Ye look that way."

El thought that the Gnome was teasing her, but she wasn't sure.

As Brytha led El out the backdoor, to a small gazebo, she said, "Don't ye worry about Vorwin. She'll get the hang of cooking for ye, and ye'll be eating better'en a king. Or a queen."

"Thanks," El said.

A Human woman sat waiting in the gazebo, a teapot and two cups before her. The woman had darker hair than the children, with broad streaks of gray going through it. She wore a sage-green shift dress that, though simple, El knew was probably extremely expensive. A rich pearl necklace encircled her neck, and a matching bracelet hung around her right wrist.

"Let's go meet the lady," Brytha said quietly.

El wasn't sure about the worry in Brytha's tone.

Ceceline Margravine couldn't be that bad, could she?

CHAPTER SEVEN

Ceceline insisted on a handshake as part of their greeting, though El would have preferred just giving her a bowed head over clasped hands.

The Human's hand fit completely inside of hers, and struck her as both limp and damp. She resisted wiping her own hand on her robe afterward.

Just barely.

El sat herself across the table from Ceceline and accepted the cup of tea that the mistress poured for her without asking.

"Well, I can see why Gyles hired you so fast," she said dryly.

El merely raised an eyebrow, encouraging the other woman to continue. Surely Ceceline didn't think her husband had hired El just because of how she looked. While all Elves were considered beautiful by Human standards, El knew that she wasn't ravishing, unlike her cousin Nadiser who'd been called the Jewel of the North.

"He said you have some teaching experience?" Ceceline said.

"Yes, a bit," El said. "I've taken care of my cousins, teaching them sums and their letters. Plus history. And I am fluent in both High Elvish and Dwarvish, and I have a solid base of Gnomish."

"More than I expected, given your looks," Ceceline admitted.

El forced herself to remain calm, serenely smiling at the Human, instead of bristling at her.

"Can you can read and write in those languages?" Ceceline said.

"Of course," El said. "And do some upper level geometry." The proper placement of siege towers and barrier walls had been drilled into her at an early age.

"Good, good," Ceceline said, looking relieved. "And you won't be casting magic all the time, right?"

"No, ma'am," El said. She held up her arm one more time. "I have no Mage Mark. I cannot cast complicated spells, or ones that are chanted." She thought again about the boy in the market, and the spells he'd cast. She was certain he didn't have enough training or power to do that level of magic without using his amulet.

What happened if he tried something more complicated? Would the spell even work?

"Good, good," Ceceline said. "I know the children are curious about you, where you come from, what type of magic you can do. Teaching them about your homeland will make for some good lessons. Without the magic, of course."

"Of course," El said, though internally, she couldn't help but roll her eyes.

Ice Elves lived in beautiful, glowing caves filled with

magic. Talking about her home without mentioning magic was going to be difficult.

"And you understand that this is just a temporary position, right?" Ceceline said. "That it's just for three months? Their regular tutor, Finmore, has traveled to see his family for the summer. And his replacement had an accident?"

"I do," El said. "I only arrived in Osirholm yesterday. Having a place to live, and something to do, while still exploring and finding my way here, seems perfect. Plus, not having to immediately commit to a long-term position suits me better."

It really was the ideal setup. Hopefully, the actual work would turn out to be just as ideal.

"That's good," Ceceline said. She seemed a bit deflated.

Had she expected El to argue with her about the terms El had already agreed to? Or had she been prepared to fight to get El to leave?

Ceceline took a sip of her tea, nodded, and said, "Right. Let's talk about the children. Sigder is ten, and Wyne is eight."

El hid her smile by taking her own sip of tea. She'd guessed their ages right. Then she focused on the tea itself. It held a smoky flavor that she found delightful, along with a sweeter note underneath. Were there berries in this tea?

She really needed to learn more about food and tastes.

"Sigder is a good boy, but lazy. Easily distracted. You'll have to come up with creative lessons to keep him engaged," Ceceline said.

"Is he competitive?" El asked. "If I made it a game, would he work harder in order to win?"

"That's actually a good idea," Ceceline said, looking

thoughtful. "See if you can motivate him by competing against himself, though. Not against his sister."

El nodded, already thinking of prizes she might be able to reward Sigder with. She'd learned early on that she, herself, responded better to sweets rather than sticks.

"I know I shouldn't say this about my children. And I do love them equally. But Wyne is smarter than her brother," Ceceline said. "She enjoys reading and easily memorizes facts. She probably reads better than he does."

"Is there anything in particular that you'd like them to learn over the summer?" El asked. "I was thinking about taking them for walks, learning the names and properties of all the local flowers and trees."

Ceceline made a face at that. "While that might be nice for the occasional outing, I'd really like to see them learn High Elvish this summer. And business. Both my husband and I work. He manages the imports for many of the wine merchants and inns in the city. I handle contracts and oversee a group of scribes."

That explained why the Margravines needed a tutor and didn't bother to teach the children themselves.

"Finmore has a lot of experience with business," Ceceline added, looking down her nose at El.

Kind of an impressive feat, given that El was at least a head taller than the Human.

"It will be fun for me to learn more," El said firmly. She was already planning on asking the children to teach her what they knew, as that would both tell her where they were in terms of their knowledge, as well as help her to learn.

"All right," Ceceline said, seeming to come to a decision. "If you need anything, Brytha will be able to take care of you. The children will be waiting for you every morning after breakfast in the classroom. You'll have them for the day, including overseeing their midday meal. You'll put them into Brytha's hands come dinner, and will have the evenings off."

"That works perfectly for me," El said.

Ceceline made a face. "It was the terms that Finmore worked out with us. He encouraged us to maintain the same schedule so the children would still be used to it when he came back."

El nodded, pleased. She hoped that at the end of the summer she'd be able to meet the person who'd obviously had such a large influence on the family.

"If there isn't anything else, I'll go to the classroom, now," El said. "The children are probably waiting there for me, right?"

"Yes," Ceceline said. "And I'll make a point of being here in the mornings for the rest of the week, in case there are any problems."

"Thank you," El said, standing. She bowed her head to the woman, turned, and walked back into the house, certain that Ceceline was staring at her back the entire time.

El had the feeling that she'd dodged an arrow, that Ceceline might have been looking to retract her husband's offer of employment for the summer.

She'd have to charm the children in the meanwhile, make it so that they'd insist that she stayed.

El didn't have a clue how to do that, particularly without using any magic.

How hard could it be, though?

CHAPTER EIGHT

Sigder and Wyne were, indeed, already in the classroom, waiting for El.

The room was on the second floor of the mansion, at the front of the house. Two large windows overlooked the garden and the quiet street, making the room feel bigger than it was. As in her room, white-painted bricks made up the walls, though the gray stone floor was smoother. Obviously, the classroom was more important than the servants' quarters. Three desks took up most of the space, the larger one with its back to the windows, the other two facing it. Low shelves lined the walls, filled with books as well as with baskets that El assumed held teaching supplics.

"Good morning," El said as she came in.

Wyne had a book open at her desk, already perusing it. Was that the *Corbray's Illustrated Guide to Herbs of Annund*? Or some other weighty tome?

Sigder sketched something in a loosely bound book that he quickly closed as soon as he realized El was there.

They wore similar clothes to what she'd seen the day

before, short-sleeves shirts, shorts, and sandals, all done in tones of green and brown. Sigder's blond-brown hair was cut short around his face, while Wyne's hung down her to the middle of her back in two tight braids.

"You're supposed to be here right after breakfast," Wyne told her with disapproval, sounding very much like her mother.

"Normally, I will be," El said, maintaining her calm. "This morning, I had to move here from the inn I was staying at. As well as speak with your mother."

"Oh," Wyne said. She glanced at Sigder, who just shrugged. "I guess that's all right, then."

"I'm glad that's met with your approval," El said dryly. "What are you reading?"

Wyne held up the familiar cover of *Corbray's Illustrated Guide to Herbs of Annund*. "You said we might use it as a teaching book, so I thought I'd try to get ahead."

"That's good," El said. "And were you drawing something?" she said, turning to Sigder.

"You weren't here," he said defensively. "I can draw when I'm not supposed to be doing lessons. Or anything else," he added with a grimace.

"That sounds right to me," El said. "And you don't have to show me if you don't want to."

Sigder sat thinking for a few moments. "Mom doesn't want me to waste my time drawing. She wants me to spend more time learning how to manage a group who does drawing. And copying."

"But how will you know if they're doing it correctly if you can't do it yourself, as well?" El asked.

Sigder's eyes grew wide. "You're right! I do need to know if they're doing it right." He gave her a shy smile. "This is what I was working on." He opened his sketchbook to the page he'd been drawing.

The half-finished pencil sketch showed Wyne sitting in the gazebo that El had seen that morning, intently reading something. The base of the building held mere suggestions of the flowers there. Only part of Wyne had been shaded and filled in, the rest of her body merely an outline.

"This is quite good!" El said.

Sigder shrugged. "It's just for fun," he said with a sigh.

El had the impression that he'd spend all his time drawing if he could. Just as Wyne might spend her days reading.

"Can you draw?" she said, turning to Wyne.

"Stick figures," she said with a grin. "I'll leave the true art to the maestro."

Sigder just rolled his eyes. It appeared to be a common tease between the two.

As drawing wasn't a skill that the Margravines were concerned about, El merely nodded. She'd have to make sure to give Sigder time to draw when she could.

"Can you two show me around the classroom? Point out what I might need?" she said. She figured asking the children to help would be the best way to start their engagement. And if they led her astray, as children were wont to do, she could figure things out herself later.

Wyne and Sigder got up from their desks and walked her around the room, pulling out baskets to show her slate boards and chalk for doing sums on, sketch books for practicing their letters and their writing, history books that they both assured her were so boring she'd never have problems falling asleep, as well as some business books of equal heft and dullness. There were also a couple of basic primers on High Elvish, but nothing on either Dwarvish or Gnomish.

"I'll have to look at the books later tonight," El told them. "Right now, I'd like to see where you are in terms of sums and maths." It would be easier for her to start with something solid, something she knew about.

Neither of the children seemed thrilled about that, but El really did need to know where they were at currently so she could figure out what she needed to teach them next. She'd learned a lot of geometry when fighting demons, particularly when it came to building adequate defenses and guard towers.

As Ceceline had told her, though Wyne was two years younger than her brother, she was his equal when it came to sums and doing fractions. She excelled at classwork, while Sigder didn't appear to be motivated. Not even by sibling rivalry.

Then El spent some time testing where they were in their language skills. Neither of them were conversant in High Elvish, just able to say a few basics, and had a rudimentary grasp of its grammar.

Just as El finished up with the tests, someone knocked on the door of the classroom.

"Hullo," said a deep male voice as a Human stuck his head around the door. "Brytha sent me to tell the young'uns that the midday meal is ready."

El tried not to stare at the man, though it was difficult. While most of his head was bald, there were still patches filled with short black hairs in random spots. Large, round ears stuck out on either side, like pitcher handles. A big nose spread across his face, with thick lips and droopy eyebrows. Pale blue eyes blinked at her, sleepy looking. He looked more like a caricature of a person, rather than an actual being.

"Thanks, Henry!" Sigder said, already out from behind his desk and racing toward the door, Wyne on his heels.

Henry came all the way into the room. "Hullo. I'm Henry," he said, "gardener and general handyman." He wore a faded gray shirt, brown pants with dirt stains on them, and scuffed black boots that should have been replaced a few years back. Either he didn't make enough money from the Margravines, which El doubted, or he wasn't bothered by his appearance.

He held out his hand, obviously intending to exchange a handshake.

El sighed but reached out and grasped Henry's hand. Though it was big and meaty, it was also very strong and calloused. Capable, despite his goofy looks. At least it was also dry, and he didn't try to overpower her.

"I'm Elbriarien," she said. "You can call me El. I'm the tutor for the summer."

"Brytha said ye'd be needing a chair for sitting in yer room," Henry said with a nod. "I got a rocker I was fixing. That do?"

"It would," El said. It wouldn't be ideal, as rockers were generally for mothers with newborn children, at least among the Ice Elves. Still, it would be better than nothing.

"I'll bring it as soon as it's done," Henry said. "If ye be needing something, something fixing or needs building, ye just give ol Henry a holler. Got that?"

"I do," El said. While he seemed a bit slow, she was certain that the Margravines wouldn't hire anyone who wasn't up to snuff.

Including herself.

El followed Henry down to the kitchen, only to be shooed outside by Brytha, as lunch was being served in the gazebo that day.

While the Ice Elves tended to eat their heaviest meal at night, here, the midday meal was the largest. Vorwin served freshly baked sourdough bread with soft cheese, followed by a delicious onion soup. Then came a course of meat that El couldn't identify, something heavy and sharply spiced, though she suspected it was some sort of pork. Vorwin served starchy root vegetables after that, as well as a type of pickled cabbage that El found delicious. Sweet glazed rolls made up the last course, which El suspected Vorwin had bought from the market rather than making them from scratch.

El tried not to yawn after such a large meal. Sleeping during the heat of the day made much more sense now if people tended to eat so much midday. Vorwin assured her that there would be a lighter meal at the end of the day, leftovers usually.

The children were lethargic after lunch, and El felt stifled as well. She assumed that Finmore didn't allow the kids to nap, though she was tempted.

"All right," El said after breaking up *another* squabble between the siblings. "We should go out for a walk or something. Bring the flower book, please, Wyne."

The kids quickly followed her out of the stuffy classroom and into the back garden. El walked with them among the flowerbeds, pointing out the flowers she could identify (which weren't many) and having the children tell her about what was there. Wynn, of course, excelled at this as well.

El encouraged Sigder to talk about how he would draw each blossom, which parts would be easy to draw and which would be difficult.

Much later, after Vorwin served them a delicious tart drink she called lemonade, El and the children went back to the classroom. She'd decided to tackle some of the lessons about business for the rest of afternoon. She got them each to talk about how to start a business, for example, selling lemonade. How would they go about doing that?

While Sigder knew about getting supplies for their shop, such as a fruit called a lemon, water, a sweetener, as well as vessels for making and serving the drink, Wyne was all about how to advertise and to start spreading the word of such a shop. Sigder came up with a logo they would put on their sign—not a lemon, because, as El pointed out, not everyone would know what that was—but a tall glass of lemonade. Even if people didn't know what it was, they would still know that it was a drink, and that the business sold drinks.

El was impressed with their knowledge of building a business. They knew a lot more of the ins and outs than she'd ever considered. She was going to have to do a lot of reading of those dubious business books to even hope to catch up with them.

When the siblings wore down on the topic of their own shop, El declared a free hour, where they could do what they would like.

Wyne promptly got out the flower book and started reading more in it. After a few moments, Sigder shyly brought out his sketch book and started sketching some of the flowers they'd looked at that afternoon.

El picked up some of the business books and started reading. The three of them were all deeply engaged when Brytha stuck her head in the classroom.

"Are they treating ye right?" she asked with an amused smile thrown at El.

"Eh, they'll do," El teased.

Both Wyne and Sigder looked affronted at her assessment.

"Figured I'd take 'em off yer hands early today. Going to market." Brytha paused. "Unless ye'd like to join us?"

El shook her head. "Another time," she said. She really would enjoy going to the market with Brytha, to see her bargain. For now, she was too tired to get much enjoyment out of the experience.

"Off with ye," El said to the kids in a fair imitation of Brytha's accent. The two scampered out of the classroom and El took a deep breath.

The first day hadn't gone too badly. They were bright kids. El wasn't certain she agreed with their mother's assessment of their intelligence. While Wyne had a higher level of book learning, Sigder was far from stupid. He was just interested in different things.

If he hadn't been the eldest son, but a second or third son, maybe he would have been allowed to go into art, to do drawing and painting. However, El understood that his parents would never allow that. He was destined for business, and his drawing would always have to be a side interest.

El would still encourage his interest in art, though. Along with Wyne's curiosity about the living world.

El picked up one of the business books that looked the least odious—*Klarner's Business ABCs*—and made her way back to her room.

A beautiful wooden rocker now sat at the foot of the bed. Mustard colored cushions had been tied to both the back and the seat. El found that it had been precisely placed so it was easy for her to look out the windows, onto the greenery behind the mansion.

She collapsed into the chair and closed her eyes. She didn't quite sleep, but did doze for a bit, resting until she heard Vorwin ring the bell for dinner. El was able to take a plate to her room and didn't have to eat with the rest of the servants. She tried reading the business book but found it went from one extreme to the other—either too simple or paragraphs filled with terms she didn't understand. The author assumed the reader had a lot more background in business than she had for the most part.

Sleep came quickly, and though El didn't feel settled, she did feel as though there was finally a new pattern to her days forming.

Hopefully the morning would bring another grand day.

CHAPTER NINE

A few nights later, after sending the children to their evening meal, El found herself too restless to stay in her room and read after dinner. She decided she needed to stretch her legs and walk more around the city. Besides, her bed held no appeal—it was far too soft.

She asked Brytha about markets on the fourth tier, but had been told that the closer to the harbor, the cheaper the prices.

So El decided to go back down to the third tier, to the night market there. Plus, she wanted to talk with Frysa and ask if any progress had been made about finding the young man who'd been casting spells. She'd described him to the Merchants' Guild guards who'd come to find her the day before, so at least she knew that it was being taken seriously.

The stairs from the fourth tier to the third were brightly lit from underneath with magical light, making it easy for El to travel down them. She could see quite well in the dark, but she was aware that not all the races had that ability.

As before, she heard and smelled the market long before

she reached it. This time, instead of the delightful chicken skewers, she got herself what was called a rice stick: sticky, sweet rice served in a short, hollow piece of bamboo, with raisins and other dried fruits mingled together. Another piece of wood pushed the rice out of the tube, making it a convenient walking-around food.

El nibbled her treat as she slowly made her way from one end of the market to the other. Most of the same vendors were there, but she still saw things she'd missed the first time she'd walked through, such as the huge woks and other cooking vessels hanging in a Dwarf's shop, a Gnome who had a fancy pastry stall with bread cooked into the shapes of frogs and other critters, plus a collection of finely polished stones with holes that could be used for stringing necklaces or bracelets from a Human's stall. She'd have to tell the children about those, and challenge them with setting up a jewelry store.

Finally, El made her way back to Frysa's stall. The Human female stood behind her table chatting with her neighbor, but greeted El with delight. Her kinky curls had been straightened some, and were now glossy waves across her scalp. Dark eyes twinkled at El from her brown face.

"The guards stopped and questioned a young man who matched your description!" Frysa said excitedly.

"And?" El said. Had they caught him?

"Before they could grab him, he disappeared. Magic," Frysa said, emphasizing the last word.

El nodded, disappointed. "I see." The young man now knew that they were onto him and would be more cautious in the future. Possibly even wearing a magical disguise. "Do they know who he is, or at least have a name for him?"

Frysa shook her head. "No, they don't. But they're now

circulating the sketch and his description on all the tiers. Someone will see him and notify the guard."

El wasn't as certain as Frysa, but then again, she'd never lived in a city that was mostly made up of Humans. Elves were good at disguises, and could easily change their appearance. Maybe since the boy wasn't naturally magical, the guards would have an easier time with it.

"How is the teaching going?" Frysa asked.

"Well, I think," El said. "The children are bright. And eager, at least some of the time."

"Coming up with interesting lessons must be challenging," Frysa said. "I know as a child I didn't always care what a teacher had to say."

"Too many other things to do," El said, nodding. It wasn't that she'd been a bad student. She was an Elf, and studious was her nature. However, she had never done as well in class as others. Learning the ancient history of the Elves had never captured her attention.

"I agree. I was always more interested in playing outside, or watching my grandma bake," Frysa said.

"So you started baking young?" El asked.

"Aye. My mum wasn't that great at it, but her mother had the touch. I'd rather have lessons from her any day."

El wished that she'd found a passion for her life. Though she'd enjoyed teaching, she knew it wasn't what she wanted to dedicate time to outside of this job. Fighting demons hadn't really been her thing either.

What did she want to do when she grew up?

A question for another day.

"Hmmm," El said. "That kind of plays into what I was considering. I want to start taking the children on field trips.

Their parents want them to learn about business. I was thinking about bringing them down to the market sometime, so they could interview some of the merchants, find out about their various businesses."

Making the business lessons directly apply to real life had been the most instructive, both for the kids and El.

"That's a great idea!" Frysa said. "Every business has its own quirks, as well as structure. Giving them real-life examples to study will really help them learn."

They quickly made plans for an afternoon meeting the following day. Frysa promised to not only explain her own process, from suppliers to selling, but also some free samples of her wares for them to sample.

"Now, this won't be a proper baking test," Frysa warned. "But one of the things that a good baker has to determine is which goods are the highest quality and should be sold at a premium, and which are for everyday use."

"I'm sure I'll fail that part," El said, laughing. "I can only grade types of lake kelp."

Frysa grinned at her. "You might surprise yourself."

A new customer came up, and El stepped back, watching how Frysa handled him, talking him into an extra roll to break his fast in the morning.

El shook her head. She was no saleswoman. She had no idea how to talk someone into anything. It was hard enough getting the children she was supposedly teaching to listen. She'd resorted to bribes get them to pay attention sometimes. Fortunately, they appeared to enjoy her singing to them in Elvish, so she used that on occasion for a reward.

El said her goodbyes to Frysa and wandered through the night market one more time, marking businesses that she thought the children might enjoy at some point. She didn't want to overload them, but perhaps a weekly trip to the market might prove productive.

CHAPTER TEN

El considered the two loaves of bread that Frysa had put on the table in front of her and the children. They were both hand shaped and round. Each would completely fill the palm of El's large, long-fingered hand.

"Which one will sell for more?" Frysa asked.

"The one on the left," Wyne answered immediately.

Sigder nodded slowly. "Yeah. Left."

El shook her head, considering the two loaves. "The one on the right," she said. Not just because she was being obstinate and didn't want to go along with everyone else. No, really. That wasn't her nature. But because that was what she thought.

"Why?" Frysa said, asking El first.

"It's more evenly baked," she said. That much, even she could see. The one on the right had a golden crust all the way around. The color on the left looked a little lighter on the side that was closest to them, while darker on the other side.

"Why did you choose the other one?" Frysa asked Wyne.

"Because the flour is more finely milled. Even though it

isn't baked as well, that flour would make it more expensive," Wyne explained.

Now that El was looking more carefully, she could see what Wyne meant. The one on the left had a finer, more smooth crust.

"That makes that much of a difference?" El asked, skeptical. "Even with the uneven bake?"

"It does," Frysa said. "A baker worth their salt wouldn't put out an inedible loaf. Slightly unevenly baked, yes. Sometimes the oven gods aren't working in your favor. However, the flour alone would still set the price higher. Even if a baker discounted it due to the bake."

"Interesting," El said, nodding. She was always learning so much!

Frysa cut open both loaves to let them taste while she talked about the different price points of various flours, how the most expensive flour wasn't always the best. (Frequently, it went rancid quicker, so you couldn't buy it and hold onto it for a special occasion—it had to be used up right away.) In addition, she covered operational costs, such as replacing equipment regularly, even pans that would degrade over time and start to burn every loaf.

Wyne and Sigder drank it in like sponges. El, too, though she wasn't sure how much of what she learned she'd ever apply.

Maybe, though, once summer was over...

She still didn't know what she was going to do.

Both the loaves were delicious, of course, as was everything that Frysa baked. However, El could tell the difference between the "mouth-feel" of the two immediately, the finer flour making the dough softer.

She wasn't about to tell Frysa, or the children, that she preferred the chewier, nuttier flavor of the less expensive loaf.

Later that evening, Brytha came knocking on El's door. "The mistress wants to see ye," she said, sounding apologetic.

El sighed, put the book she'd been trying to get through aside (really, the children were right, most of these books worked best as sleep aids) and went down the back staircase to the study that stood beside Gyles's.

El hadn't been invited into either study. The glance she'd gotten of Gyles's was that it was very masculine, with the heavy, dark wood furniture that seemed to be the style of the entire house.

It surprised her, then, that Ceceline's study was very feminine. The wooden chairs were lighter in color, the wood not as thick, and covered in pastel-colored cushions. Her desk stood clear of any papers or files. Only a beautiful cut-glass pen-and-ink stand decorated it. Instead of dark wood bookshelves, Ceceline's were all painted white.

The room reflected a lighter mood than El thought Ceceline ever exhibited.

Ceceline stared at El with cool gray eyes, the corners of her mouth turned down. She wore another "simple" dress, done in pastel blue.

Were the lighter colors supposed to mask how intense this woman actually was?

El wasn't about to ask what Ceceline wanted—the woman had called for El to come and see her, not the other way around.

Finally, Ceceline spoke. "The children told me about the outing you took them on this afternoon."

El nodded, smiling. "Yes. I thought it was good for them to

learn about business from other business owners. Real-life examples are a good teacher." Plus, the children had been eager to discuss how they would run their own bake shop, the clientele they'd wish to attract, the sorts of goods they might serve. It had led to a long discussion on taxes, and how various products were or were not taxed. What was considered regular food—a staple—had no tax on either it or the goods to produce it. While a luxury food—such as the finer bread and its flour—would be taxed.

Ceceline frowned. "While I approve of the idea, really, you need to take them to proper stores. Not common businesses. They aren't going to be responsible for a simple market stall. There are economies of scale that they need to learn about, and that only comes with a bigger enterprise."

"Oh," El said, blinking. She'd never thought of that, how a small business might differ from a bigger one. "Still, isn't it better that they learn all the various types of business? Both big and small? In case they want to start their own side business while still running a larger company?"

That appeared to be the right thing to say, as Ceceline gave her a tight smile. "I suppose you're right, that they should learn about businesses big and small. But please, do shift your focus to stores, not stalls."

"I can do that," El said, nodding. She wasn't sure if that was a dismissal or not, as Ceceline continued to stare at her.

"How is it going?" she finally asked.

"Good," El said. "Wyne definitely has a head for numbers, while Sigder excels at languages. They both understand the basics of business, supply chains, profit and loss. I've learned a lot working with them."

"I see," Ceceline said. "Though you are teaching them, right?"

"I am," El said. "I've been studying ahead so I can

continue to bring new business concepts to them. I've had them develop their own small businesses, pointing out the variables they haven't thought of after they determine their concept."

"Sounds like a solid way to engage them," Ceceline said, finally approving.

"If there isn't anything else?" El asked, half-rising.

Ceceline appeared to think for a moment before she shook her head. "No, that's all. Just make sure that they're learning business from both big and small leaders in our community."

"Yes, ma'am," El said cheerfully as she made her way out of the study and back up to her room.

She sagged against the door after she closed it, feeling as though she'd just had a narrow escape. At least she was doing what Ceceline Margravine wanted in general terms of giving lessons to her children.

But how was she going to find a bigger shop keeper who would be willing to talk to the kids?

Maybe Frysa would know someone...

Or better yet, Kucher.

CHAPTER ELEVEN

El herded the children toward the steps to go back up to the fourth tier after they'd had another successful business learning session. This time it had been in a "proper" shop—a bag maker who Frysa had introduced El to. The woman had been tickled to talk about her business, taking delight in how she managed her relationships with the actual creators of the bags, striving to get the best price for everything she sold. It wasn't enough that made a profit, no, she was committed to making sure the artisans she worked with also received a living wage.

"Can we stop and get an ice? With berries? Please?" Wyne asked before they reached the stairs.

El had no idea what they were talking about. She let them lead her along the main street, then down a side-street to a small, two-story shop that had a sign outside that said:

Ice & Berries
Finest snowy treats around!

Kucher hadn't taken her to this shop, or even down this street. El shook her head. She really needed to start exploring more on her own.

But what in the world was a snowy treat? And why would anyone want to eat snow? Or ice, for that matter?

A cheery bell rang as Wyne pushed the door open. The store was larger than El had thought. It ran the entire depth of the building, with a wide aisle filled with white iron chairs and clean white tables for customers heading straight back from the door. To the right was another, wider area filled with more customer seating. Past those, long counters with chairs lined the center area. Nothing adorned the walls, and a very pale wood covered the floor. It pleased her how cold the place felt, as though she'd just stepped into a refreshing ice cave.

Behind the counters stood a large machine, painted bright red with delicate blue filigree lines decorating it—the only color in the entire place. It was as tall as El, maybe four feet long and three across.

El gasped and stopped, though the children plowed straight ahead, leaning on the counter like they owned the place.

That was a Dwarven war machine, designed to produce ice and snow to fight demons.

What was it doing here?

Slowly, El moved forward, her focus on the machine. The front of it had been greatly modified. Instead of a single large opening that would shoot out a winter storm, there were three silver spigots, each about the size of her palm. Knobs, buttons, and dials adorned the space above and below them.

When El got to the counter, she realized that just past the flat surface stood a small container, maybe two foot by three foot, packed with snow. A few bottles and some small closed pails stuck out of the snow.

Was this how the owner kept them cold? Why didn't they just use magic, if they had a Dwarven war machine?

Finally, El took in the person chatting with the children.

She wasn't an Elf. And she certainly wasn't a Dwarf or a Gnome, given how she probably came up to El's shoulder. In fact, El didn't feel any magic emanating from her at all. She presented as Human.

However, she was ethereally beautiful. Golden skin covered her thin face, with classically high cheekbones, a pointed nose, and sharp chin. Amber eyes holding weighty sorrow still lit up as she answered the children's questions. Her auburn hair fell in soft waves to her shoulders, held back by delicate gold and silver butterflies.

El shook her head, realizing that she was staring. Not only that, this person had asked her a question and she hadn't heard a word due to the pounding of her blood in her ears.

"Excuse me?" El said. She didn't blush. Elves didn't allow themselves that sort of reaction.

Still. El felt her cheeks grow slightly warm as she gazed into the honeyed eyes of the store's owner. Must be the heat coming from the machine. Yeah, that was it.

"As I was explaining to the young ones, I'll do my best to make ye ices. But the beast here has been cranky all morning."

"Beast?" El asked, slightly alarmed as she looked the shop.

"No, lass, not a real one. Just this critter, here. Nilafels," the shop owner said, patting the war machine fondly.

She had a strange accent. El would say that she sounded

more Dwarf than Human, though her voice was melodic and smooth.

"What's it doing?" El asked.

The shop owner paused and looked El up and down before responding. "Eh, at times, the ice flows as it should. Other times, it just spits out dribbles. Like today."

"Can I...can I take a look?" El said, her gaze recaptured by the machine.

"Do ye think ye can help?" the shop owner asked, a little suspicious.

"I used to work with machines like this. Back in my homeland," El said. "I'm an Ice Elf."

The shop owner looked El up and down again, her eyes widening before she nodded.

"Please, then. Come on back," the shop owner said. She opened up a portion of the counter so El could slip through.

Had this beast, this Nilafels, ever seen combat? El wasn't sure. The exterior seemed too pristine, not scratched and dinged from being carted from one battleground to the next.

Then again, maybe the exterior had been refurbished when the other adjustments to it had been made.

El slowly placed her hands on the machine, one on the side and the other on the back. Then she let her awareness seep into the hard metal. She'd been taught to do this early on, to sense the magic in the machines, in case she needed to work with one at the end of a battle when all her spell ingredients had been used up.

The machine wasn't identical to the ones she'd used up north. No, this had been specifically modified so that someone non-magical could use it. A large pan at the back held water, which was fed through the freezing mechanism, then forced out the spigots on the face of the machine. The act of water being poured in activated the machine and kick-started the magical mechanisms it contained.

El found the problem quickly. A large piece of enchanted metal at the foot of the machine—part of the apparatus for freezing the water—had frozen solid. Only dribbles of water were able to get through.

It took a quick flick of her own magic to clear the blockage.

"I've never seen Nilafels light up that way," the shop owner said as El stepped back. She sounded envious.

The blue filigreed design on the side of the machine now glowed with ice magic.

El just shrugged. "Should be working now."

"What was the problem?" the shop owner asked, still curiously aggrieved.

El explained, then added, "You need to make sure to power down the machine at night. That way, any moisture inside Nilafels won't freeze."

"Hmm," the golden woman said. "I'll check me notes. Thatur must have left instructions for that. I'm Mara, by the way. Mara Fane."

El introduced herself and the children.

"So what do you make here? Exactly?" El had to ask.

"This here's the best shaved ice in town!" Mara exclaimed enthusiastically.

At El's blank look, Mara continued. "Nilafels produces three different types of ice: crushed, flaked, and shaved. Crushed is the most chunky, shaved is the most smooth. People compare it to eating snow."

"And?" El said after a few moments.

"Then you add flavorings to it," Mara said proudly, indicating the container with all the bottles and pots. "Such as Dragonberry, Cave Jasmine, or even Goldenhorn Delight!"

"My favorite is the Cloud Apricot," Wyne said.

"I like the Silver Pineapple," Sigder added.

El peered at the myriad offerings. There wasn't a menu she could look at. She just had to remember what Mara said when she listed off flavors, though most of them meant nothing to her.

"I...I don't like things that are too sweet," El said after a moment, while they were all looking at her expectantly. She only ever took a mouthful of any of Vorwin's desserts.

"Just the thing, then," Mara said. She held up a bottle that was a peculiar reddish-green.

While the color made El smile, the children both said, "Ewww." But to El, it resembled one of her favorite pickled vegetables from home.

"Saffron Moss," Mara announced.

"Ew," the children said again, making faces.

El nodded, agreeing to try it, though she still had no idea what that was going to taste like.

Mara turned to Nilafels and poured water into the back from a full bucket. The machine made a peculiar chugging sound as the magic started. Even though El was no longer touching the machine, she could still sense how the water moved along, activating sigils as it flowed from one part to the next.

Sigder ordered the chunkier ice, so he could chew on it, while Wyne had asked for the flaked, and El had gone for the smoothest, wondering what exactly eating snow would be like. Snow that wasn't really snow.

Mara filled three bowls with ice from the three different

spigots, added drizzles of toppings, then handed them to her guests with spoons. "Enjoy!"

El glanced at the three dishes. Wyne's—the Cloud Apricot—had a whitish yellow color. Though it had artful swirls over it, it still looked like snot to her. Sigder's was bright silver that looked metallic and not necessarily appealing, while her own was a peculiar red-green that had her questioning her choice.

"How much?" El asked, reaching for the money bag tied to her waist.

"Free," Mara said firmly. "Ye fixed Nilafels, here. I owe you."

"But we're getting free product," El said, feeling stubborn. She'd learned too much about business to feel good about taking anything without paying for it. While the ice probably didn't cost anything, the syrups and various berries were probably very expensive.

"Ya, sure, but now I can serve other people. What they buy will make up for what I give to ye," Mara said, pushing the bowls toward them again. Then she stepped back and stood with her arms crossed over her chest, a stubborn look filling her elegant face.

"Fine," El said. She followed Wyne to a table that was close to one of the two windows looking over the street.

"If we sit here, where people can see us eating and enjoying ourselves, then they'll come in too," Wyne explained as she seated El with her back to the window, while she and Sigder faced her.

El tried her treat. The finely shaved ice melted in her tongue, better than snow, she thought. Though the color was slightly off-putting, it tasted both sweet and salty, a combination that El enjoyed.

Neither of the children liked her treat though. They graciously allowed her to try theirs, though theirs were both too sweet for El.

However, their plan worked, for soon someone else joined them in the shop. It was disappointing to El when it turned out to be just one other customer, who finished his ice quickly, and then left.

Something else was going on here. Why weren't more people coming in?

And who was this Mara? She looked magical, but she didn't feel magical. Was she just a Human from some other place? Or was she something else?

They left the shop, El's curiosity burning at an all-time high.

CHAPTER TWELVE

The following night, El went to *The Book Ends* inn to see if perhaps Kucher wanted to talk with Wyne and Sigder about the business he ran with Nel. He was definitely the more boisterous of the pair of them. Plus, the inn would qualify as a store and not a stall in the market, at least in El's mind. In addition, Kucher appeared to know everyone. Surely he could introduce El to some other business owners who would want to talk about their business to the children.

She didn't want to admit that she also wanted to see if she could get additional background on Mara Fane. Something about the person attracted El, made her want to question the other female and find out all about her.

She hesitated to call Mara a woman. She might be Human. She presented that way. However, El wasn't convinced, despite the lack of magical power emanating from her.

The tavern was full that night, with Nel behind the bar, Kucher serving tables, and a Human girl who El hadn't seen before helping out.

El sat up at the bar instead of at a table so she could get a quiet word in with Nel between mixing drink orders.

"Now, while I think that talking to the kids is a good idea, the Margravines might not appreciate you bringing them here," Nel warned. "They see this as a tavern, not as a proper inn. They won't want them learning this trade."

El sighed. Nel was probably right. Ceceline had made it clear that while El could continue to talk with various shop owners, she didn't necessarily approve of "common business-es." And there were taverns on practically every street.

"Here for the pub quiz?" Kucher asked as El thought about how to get around Ceceline's disapproval.

"What's a pub quiz?" El asked.

"Eh, you'll love it," Kucher assured her. "Come with me."

El picked up the lovely glass of brandy that Nel had served her and followed Kucher to a table on the side, where a female Dwarf and two male Humans were already seated. They explained how someone called a quiz master would ask questions of all sorts of topics. The team with the most correct answers would each win a free drink the next time they came in.

As El suspected, she was awful at the pub quiz, not knowing most of the answers to common questions such as the types of monsters that inhabited Grimhall Falls (cloud harpies that lived in the mists caused by the falling water), the divisions of the Gnome court (seemed they had an upper, middle, and lower elected house of commons in addition to a queen), as well as all the ingredients that made up Island Stammerwort stew (a combination of saffron, apple mint, and wild oregano, to name a few). At least El could answer the history questions, as she knew the old stories of Annund better than most.

Her team—appropriately named the Leftovers—didn't win any of the prizes. However, she did agree to bring the children to meet the Dwarf, Orin, in a few days' time to learn about the silver trade. He worked as a representative of one of the nearby mines, and negotiated deals with various craftspeople to buy their silver. It wasn't a "proper" business, as he had no shop. However, he was very familiar with contract law, and large sums of money were involved. Surely the Margravines couldn't object to either of those.

Kucher, as well, agreed to meet with her and the kids at *Ice & Berries*, to talk strictly about the inn and not how to run a tavern. Surprisingly, he knew only a little about Mara. Evidently, she'd arrived before summer the year before, the shop had been open during the hot season, then closed all winter. He hadn't heard that she'd opened again for business.

El wondered if that was it—that people just hadn't realized the shop was open again, which was why there were so few customers. Or if there was something else, some other hidden secret that she was missing.

Beside the ethereal beauty of the owner.

Maybe El could get Mara to talk about her business with the children. Kucher was certain that Mara's partner, a Dwarf named Thatur, would be able to step in and help. Or perhaps he would chat with them, while Mara ran the shop and served customers.

El nodded, though she didn't think that was possible. Hadn't Mara mentioned Thatur while they'd been in the shop, something about his notes? Perhaps the Dwarf had taken a holiday somewhere, and would be back shortly?

Still, it meant yet another opportunity to go to the shop,

to taste yet another ice, to explore the mystery that El felt was there.

The day that El and the children were to meet Kucher dawned warm, and grew much hotter as the morning progressed. El hoped that *Ice & Berries* wasn't completely packed by the time they got there. Surely there would be a line out the door, with customers all seeking something cool on such a hot day?

However, it turned out that El and the children were the only ones in the shop again.

"How is Nilafels running?" El asked as they came in.

"The wee beasty is doing fine," Mara assured her. "Want to take a look?" she asked.

El could tell that Mara was trying to be casual about her request. However, the tension in her shoulders was a serious tell.

"I'd be happy to!" El said, walking behind the counter when Mara invited her in.

Nilafels started glowing as soon as El put her hands on it. Though she didn't find an actual sentience in the machine, there did appear to be a slight awareness, as if the magic that powered the machine was pleased by her presence.

While none of the ice-making parts had frozen again, a slight build-up of ice had started forming in the pipe leading to the snow spigot. El melted that away, then dried the pipe, so that it wouldn't form again.

"Everything is in perfect running order," El assured Mara, as she didn't want to make the owner feel as though she owed anything to El.

All three of them ordered different syrups this time. El tried something called Cranberry Crane, which looked disturbingly like blood dripped on her ice. The Marsh Honey

Tart that Wyne tried was a bright yellow color. Unfortunately, it reminded El of a common warning in the north, to never eat yellow snow. The River Berry that Sigder tried was a warm brown color, looking like lumpy gravy.

Kucher was late. Fortunately, El had been forewarned by Nel about this, that while she loved her husband, he didn't have the same concept of timeliness as other people. He came bustling in after El and the children had almost finished their treats, waving at El and the kids before walking over to Mara and introducing himself. The Bouncing Lotus that he ordered for himself looked like bloody snot, but he pronounced it as divinely flavored.

Fortunately, Kucher came prepared for their lesson, and was able to walk Wyne and Sigder through all the steps in owning an inn, from choosing the location, to choosing the name (turned out the numbers carved into their sign was a street address) to monthly costs versus incidentals, when to consider hiring staff, and so on.

In addition, Kucher emphasized the importance of relationships with all the other businesses. It meant that all his acquisitions could go much more smoothly (and frequently, more cheaply) if he made friends with other shopkeepers. Or at least that was how he justified knowing at least half the people in Osirholm.

As he was finishing up with the kids, El walked back up to the counter to chat with Mara. She explained what they were doing, how she was a tutor teaching the children business for summer months.

"Would you be willing to talk with them?" El ended with, unable to keep the hopeful look out of her eyes.

"I cannot leave the shop," Mara said, looking down suddenly.

"No, we could come here. Could your partner, Thatur, look after the shop for a bit? Or maybe he could talk with us while you worked?" El said, still hopeful.

That brought Mara's eyes up.

For the first time, her gaze seemed lifeless. Hopeless. The sorrow in them wrapped around El's heart and squeezed it hard.

"Thatur Icemaster passed away this winter," Mara said, her voice losing all its melodiousness and turning monotone. "He'd never fully recovered from the...the incident. We came to the city, hoping to find a cure for the life that I...that had been stolen from him. I—we—I failed him."

"I'm so very sorry for your loss," El said. She had to physically hold herself back from reaching across the counter to squeeze one of Mara's hands.

"He knew he dinna have long," Mara said quietly. She looked to the side, then tilted her head back, to nod at Nilafels. "He created this beastie so that I could have a living without him. Though without him, it isn't much of a living."

That explained the modifications that had been made to the war machine, why it had been changed so it could work for someone without magic.

"And ye don't want me talking business, teaching business," Mara added, turning back to El, her composure mostly returned. "Ye see the number of customers I have. I'm barely making rent."

As if to dispute her words, the bell hanging over the lintel rang and a mother with two young children came in. "Oh, I'm so glad you're open today!" she called out merrily as she herded her young ones to the counter.

El walked slowly back to the table with Kucher and the children.

An idea slowly started to form about how to help Mara. And make it educational.

Hopefully, she could talk all the parties involved into seeing things her way.

CHAPTER THIRTEEN

The next morning, El did language lessons with the children in the classroom. Sigder continued to be able to speak High Elvish better than Wyne, though she had a larger vocabulary. However, she couldn't get the pronunciation on some words and she had a much more difficult time with the tones.

They were neck and neck when it came to Dwarvish. Though El didn't encourage a sibling rivalry or set them against each other, they did it themselves with certain topics.

After lunch, instead of returning to the stuffy classroom, they took refuge in the cool garden, sitting in the gazebo. El brought out chalkboards, plenty of chalk, but no books.

"So, how do you fix a failing business?" she asked, figuring that would be a good way to broach the topic.

"Depends on why it's failing," Wyne said, her expression a little cross.

"Fire everyone and start with all new help. That's what Mom always says," Sigder added.

"Wouldn't the cost of training all new staff make that costly?" El asked, unsurprised about Ceceline's approach.

That dour woman would of course want to wipe the books clean instead of trying to work with people, to improve a situation.

Sigder shrugged. "They either learn or are replaced, as they know what happened to the previous staff."

"That doesn't reward loyalty," El pointed out.

"And while that might fix the current problems, you'd have a whole new set to deal with," Wyne said, still sounding annoyed.

El didn't have any idea why the girl was so downcast, but hopefully it wouldn't interfere with their lessons that afternoon.

"So replacing everyone isn't the answer?" Sigder said, sounding confused.

"There might be instances where that is appropriate, such as if someone came in with a really bad attitude and managed to infect the rest of the staff with it," El said. "Though ideally you'd catch something like that quickly, before everyone was complaining."

"Fat chance of Mom ever doing that," Wyne said sourly. "She doesn't listen much."

El merely nodded politely and moved on. If Wyne decided to confide in her later, she'd be willing to listen. But she didn't feel as though she could pry, not at this point in her relationship with the children.

"Remember what Kucher said about relationships? That doesn't just apply to your vendors or suppliers, but also to your staff," El said.

The children nodded, as if they hadn't considered that before.

"So why is the business failing?" Wyne asked, staying on target. She could be tenacious that way. And maybe it was a way to distract herself from whatever had happened with her mother.

"What could cause a business to fail?" El said.

The children started listing off possible causes, such as wrong area of town for their goods—you wouldn't put a high-end bakery next to the piers on the first level. No one rich was going to go down that far to buy anything, and the people who lived at that level couldn't afford such goods.

El knew that *Ice & Berries* was ideally located. Sure, it wasn't on the main street, but it wasn't in a bad neighborhood. There was still plenty of foot traffic.

Another cause was competition. Perhaps there was a store just up the street that sold identical goods. The owner might get into a bidding war, which would eat into their profit.

El pointed out that in this sort of situation, staff was key. The store with the better, friendlier, more personable staff—even if it was just the owner themselves—could make all the difference. People would consider paying more for an item if they enjoyed the experience.

"Unknown products," Sigder said after a moment.

El contained her smile, thinking that he may have hit on a key point. "Go on," she encouraged. Maybe he was thinking of *Ice & Berries*, and the lack of a menu?

"Mom ran into that problem at one point," Sigder said. "Existing customers knew all the services that her shop did. New customers didn't. So they'd come in and just order one thing. The staff wasn't upselling them. So she came up with a menu board that listed all their specialties. It was a real boost to sales. Plus, once that was in place, they could run discounts that were time sensitive. Of course, she bumped up the prices two weeks before the discount, so they weren't losing that much money. But running regular sales turned some customers into repeat customers."

"Wouldn't regularly having discounts cheapen the customer relationship? Such that they would only come in during a discount?" El asked.

"It would," Sigder said, nodding sagely. "That's why the discounts are infrequent and specifically irregular. So that customers can't rely on them."

El just shook her head, marveling at how much she was learning, as well as how much the children already knew.

"So, do you think that *Ice & Berries* would benefit from a menu?" El asked, finally steering their conversation toward her end goal.

"Yes!" Wyne said, sounding happy finally. "You could draw it for them," she added, nodding at Sigder.

"That would be fun!" Sigder said.

"Plus, an illustration of what ice and berries means," El added. "Existing customers already know what they're getting. New customers don't have a clue."

"Oh, yes," Wyne said, nodding. "Mara's shop is nice, but it is a little plain. And cold. You know?"

El shrugged. She thought the lack of ornamentation and the chilled air was delightful, but not everyone shared her tastes. Brytha was always trying to get El to add more knickknacks to her room, telling her that it looked like the cell of a priestess dedicated to a particularly austere god. Vorwin claimed that lack of ornamentation was part of why El was still single and unable to attract a decent mate: not only was she skinny, but unadorned.

"What else could Mara do?" El asked.

"Change the flavors of her syrups," Wyne said. "I've tried almost all of them but there are only a few that are good."

"And the colors," Sigder added.

El merely nodded. She knew her tastes were a little different than most people's, but even she was hard pressed to find flavors she liked.

"Maybe give customers samples? So they can taste a flavor before buying it?" Sigder added. "That's something Mom does with the copies. Customers can feel what the different weights of paper are, as well as the different styles of calligraphy and copies."

"She should buy a bunch of tiny spoons," Wyne said. "And there should be a sign about a limit of three samples."

"So fill each spoon with a tiny bit of the shaved ice, with a drop of a flavor on top?" El asked.

"Exactly!" Wyne said, nodding. "I'm sure Brytha could get you the cheapest price on the spoons. Or maybe your friend Kucher." She gave El an evil grin. "Make it a competition between the pair of them."

El couldn't help but snort at that. Though Kucher was Human, he did have a Dwarvish pride in getting the best bargain.

"But then there are the flavors," El said. This was really the sticking point, for her. She knew that she couldn't judge what would be tasty for most people.

"Ask Vorwin," Sigder suggested.

"She already has so much work here, at the house. Would she have time to help us?" El asked. She'd considered the Gnome already, as Vorwin did make food that everyone else considered delicious. It was far too rich, too spicy, or too sweet for El at least half of the time.

But again, she thought pickled lake weed was an amazing delicacy.

"She might. At night," Sigder said. "She complains sometimes about cooking for such a small family."

Wyne looked at him strangely. "When do you talk with her?"

Sigder just shrugged. "I get hungry sometimes. At night. So I go looking for a snack in the kitchen. She's always there."

"She has her own room, doesn't she?" El said, starting to get alarmed.

"Yes," Sigder said. "And she's released from her duties during the Gnome holidays, so she always gets to go home and cook for her family. She just loves to cook."

El shook her head. Cooking had never been her preference. But she did know that some of her uncles, and at least one or two of her aunts, who enjoyed it.

"All right, I'll go talk with her," El said. "But we need to come up with a presentation for Mara, to get her to agree to accept our help."

"Mom always says that you never get anything for free, that you always have to pay in the end," Sigder said wisely, nodding his head. "You might get a sample, but not a lot more."

"So what would we want to charge Mara? She isn't making a lot money currently," El warned.

"We could get a share of the profits," Wyne said.

"Net profit," Sigder chimed in, "not gross. Assuming there was any profit."

"Of course," Wyne said, as if that were a given.

El smiled, pleased her charges were looking out for Mara.

"Just a small percentage," Wyne continued. "That way, if our ideas help the business, we make money. If our ideas don't work, nobody gets paid anything."

"Mom would like that too," Sigder said. "A classroom project that turned a profit would be her ideal scenario."

Wyne nodded in agreement, though a part of El was still aghast.

Couldn't learning be done just for the sake of learning? Did everything have to be money driven?

"All right, then we have our assignments," El said. "Wyne, you come up with an initial business plan and contract. We'll all go over them. Sigder, you come up with two, no, three potential menus with explanatory illustrations. After we see your initial drawings, we'll tighten up the concept and determine how many we actually want to present to Mara. In the meanwhile, I'll talk with Vorwin about berry recipes, and maybe with Brytha about supplies."

El hid her grimace. She felt like she was giving orders on a battlefield. However, the children nodded enthusiastically, quickly going to work. It was, in fact, child's play to them. They didn't have any stake in the business succeeding or failing.

Except their pride, of course, and wanting to outdo each other.

Hopefully, that would be enough to make them put forth their best effort.

CHAPTER FOURTEEN

El didn't go back down to the kitchen until a few hours after the last meal had been served. She wanted to make sure that Vorwin would have time to talk with her, before the Gnome trundled off to bed.

El hadn't been in the kitchen at night before. The hulking stove still gave off a slight glow—letting it cool down completely would mean a lot of time warming it up in the morning. All the dishes stood shining in the cupboard, the counters clean. The faint scent of the cinnamon buns that Vorwin had served after dinner lingered in the air.

Vorwin was there, as Sigder had predicted. The Gnome stood on her box at the center island table, her stubby fingers stripping leaves off dried stems. When El stepped closer, she could smell the mint.

"Good evening," Vorwin said, looking up from her work. "You come for a snack?"

She sounded so hopeful El almost didn't want to tell her no.

But she did. The Gnome's insistence on "fattening her

up" hadn't done much more than leave extra food on El's plate. She wasn't about to force herself to eat when she wasn't hungry, much to Vorwin's dismay.

"No, I'm not," El said. "Sorry," she added, feeling as though she had to.

"Fine," Vorwin said with a heavy sigh. "What do you want?"

"Are you familiar with the shop *Ice & Berries*?" El said, getting right to the point.

Vorwin's amber eyes grew thoughtful for a moment, though her hands never stopped moving. "Yeah. My cousin stopped by there once. Wasn't impressed with the flavors. Suspect they'd be something *you'd* like, though."

El smiled at the teasing. "Actually, Mara only has one flavor that I enjoy," she said honestly.

"All right," Vorwin said. She seemed surprised at El's statement.

"So as part of a classroom project, I'm having Wyne and Sigder come up with a business plan and other things to help Mara and the shop," El explained.

"I'm listening," Vorwin said, suddenly sounding cautious.

"While the children and I believe we can come up with solid steps to help Mara, none of us are cooks. We can't create new recipes that Mara can use on the ices," El admitted.

Vorwin snorted but didn't say anything.

"The children suggested that I ask you if you could help, at least to initially develop some new flavors, that would taste better, that Mara could easily make," El said. "New syrups that wouldn't take too much time to make, with affordable ingredients."

"What's in it for me?" Vorwin asked immediately. "This

isn't a classroom project for me. This is taking up my spare time. What do I get?"

"I don't know," El said. She'd been hoping that Vorwin would see this as a challenge and volunteer her time. She should have known better.

Everyone in the Margravines employment had a better business sense than she did.

"Free ices for life," Vorwin tossed out over her shoulder.

El blinked. That would probably actually work. Vorwin didn't leave the kitchen much, so she probably wouldn't be able to abuse her free ice privilege.

"Okay," El said after a few moments.

With a heavy sigh, Vorwin slammed the stem she'd been working on down on the table. "No, no, no! That's not how it goes at all."

"I'm sorry?" El said, unsure of what Vorwin meant.

The Gnome faced her, her stubby arms bent and her fat hands folded into fists, jammed into the location where her waist probably was.

"Look! That's not how it's done," Vorwin said. "Here, I'll show you." She cleared her throat, then said in a forceful voice, "I want free ices for life."

Then Vorwin climbed off her box, came to stand in front of El, deliberately turning her back to her.

"That's totally unreasonable!" Vorwin said, her voice lilting and high.

Wait, was that supposed to be an imitation of El?

"We'd go broke if we had to give you all your ices for free, particularly for the rest of your long and prosperous life. How about one free ice per month, for a year?"

Vorwin stomped back to her box and glared at El. "One free ice per month? For only a year?" she said, sputtering.

"Do you not value me or my input? Are you trying to put my work to shame? How dare you insult me, my family name, and my reputation this way! One free ice per week, for life."

Vorwin got off her box again, walking over to El and turning her back on the Elf again, as if she was continuing the conversation with an imaginary person on the box.

"If you're so insistent on this 'for life' nonsense," Vorwin said, again, with that silly, high-pitched voice she was using, "then why don't we agree to do additional flavors for life as well? Not a one-time duty, but ongoing? So one free ice per season, for life. But that also means new flavors every season."

El finally saw the strategy in that. Making Vorwin a part of the shop's continued existence would mean that the shop would have a much better chance of survival. Still, did El really sound like that? With such a high voice?

Vorwin marched back to her box and turned to face El, armed crossed over her broad chest.

"One free ice per week, along with three new flavors per season," Vorwin said. "And that's my final offer."

The Gnome stayed where she was on the box, glaring at El, daring her to come up with a better offer.

"I'll take it?" El said, wondering if that was the appropriate response.

Before Vorwin could abuse her anymore, El added, "And I'll have Wyne draw up the contract."

Vorwin's eyes narrowed at that. "Good. She's better at that sort of thing than Sigder. Boy's a wonder, but he has too soft of a heart."

El shook her head. She wasn't sure about that, but she'd take Vorwin's word for it.

"Are we done here? Because I've got to get cooking," Vorwin said with a gleam in her eye.

"Before you've signed a contract?" El said, surprised.

"Eh, those are just details. I have ideas that I want to try, first," Vorwin said.

El opened her mouth then shut it again. Vorwin had been looking for a challenge, something more to do. At least that was the impression that Sigder had given her, and that Vorwin had just solidified.

"Thank you," El said sincerely. "For the lesson in bargaining, as well as agreeing."

Vorwin waved her thanks away before she pulled out a small pot and reached for her herbs.

El knew better than to stand in the way of a creative genius at work.

Now, all they had to do was to convince Mara that they could actually help.

CHAPTER FIFTEEN

It took the better part of a week for them to finalize everything—the business plan, the contracts, the menus and other helpful signage, along with the flavors that Vorwin was proposing. The children had been most excited about that aspect, as it meant they had to taste all of the various concoctions that Vorwin came up with, though without ice.

Her arms full of papers, sauce jars in a bag, El stepped into *Ice & Berries* just as the shop was about to close.

No customers were in the shop, and Mara appeared to be shutting down the great war machine Nilafels. She'd removed the basin at the back of it, where she would generally add water, and was drying it off.

"We're closed—oh! Hello. Nice to see ye," Mara said. At least she brightened up when she saw that it was El who'd just rung the doorway bell. Then Mara looked down at the basin in her arms. "Sorry, lass. But I don't have any ice for ye. I'm just closing shop."

"Good," El said, walking toward the back and setting down her armful of papers on one of the tables, then starting to spread them out onto two others. "I didn't want to bother you, or to come earlier, in case you were busy. But I have a proposition for you. Several, in fact."

"All right then," Mara said, sounding perplexed. "Just a moment and I'll be right there."

She finished wiping down the basin before putting it back into Nilafels, closing the door firmly. She gave a final loving wipe of her cloth to the side of the machine before she lifted up a part of the counter and walked to the tables where El was waiting.

El stayed standing. It was only then, when Mara came to stand directly beside her, that she realized that Mara was exactly the same height as her. Mara tended to stay crouched over, minimizing her tallness.

Had this been because her partner, Thatur, had been a Dwarf?

The warmth that El felt came from Mara herself. It was as if she was standing next to a warm hearth after being outside on a cold, blustery day.

"So what's this then?" Mara asked, glancing down at the menus and instructional aids that El had spread out over two of the tables, with a curious glance at the third, where the contracts sat.

"As I told you before, I'm teaching business to the children for the summer," El said. "I know it was presumptuous of me, but you did mention that you were struggling. So the children and I came up with a business plan to help turn the shop around."

She pointed to the four small jars containing the sauces that Vorwin had come up with. "We have new business concepts, new menus, new flavors."

Mara's mouth was open as she looked at the drawings, the jars, up to El, then back again.

"The contracts propose a profit-sharing agreement, to allow us to help you and for the arrangement to be mutually beneficial," El said, pointing to the third table where the contracts awaited. "Plus another, separate contract for creating new flavors once a season, depending on local fruit and other resources." That had been one of the items that Vorwin had negotiated fiercely for, that most of the syrups be made out of fresh fruit.

Mara looked again at everything. Her fingers traced the beautiful scroll work that Sigder had added to the top of the menu. Berries hung from it, and snowflakes dotted the sides of it.

"I accept," Mara said with a shaky voice.

"Uhm, you, uhm, need to read the contracts," El said hurriedly. "I don't want you to feel as though we're forcing you into some sort of unfair deal."

Mara's laughter rung out, clear as bells on a cold winter day. "Oh, lass, I know yer not. And yes, we'll negotiate some, for me pride if nothing else. But all I can say is thank you. We'll make it work."

Then she turned, her amber eyes burning with an internal fire. "But what are ye getting out of it?" she asked quietly, her eyes searching El's. "Whatever reason could such a marvelous person as yerself want to help?"

"You," El breathed out, hypnotized by the warmth that seemed to emanate from Mara. Then she caught herself, realizing what she'd just said. "I don't mean it that way," El said, taking a step back. "Just that—I get to help you. That's it."

Oh gods. Ice Elves did *not* blush. No matter how fair their skin was. They just didn't do that.

But El's cheeks felt unusually warm, gazing at Mara.

Mara gave her a quizzical look. "I'm nothing special," she said as she looked away.

"Don't say that," El said.

If she dared more, she would have reached across the icy gulf separating them, turning Mara's gaze back toward her, to bask again in that warmth.

She didn't dare.

"Don't lie to me," El added as Mara continued to not meet her eye. "You're special. A person just has to look at you to know that."

Mara's laugh was equal parts bitter and exasperated. "Not special enough," she said cryptically as she looked back at El, her gaze less personal, the warmth replaced with Mara's usual sadness. "Let's take a look at the contracts then, shall we?"

"Aren't you curious about the new flavors we're suggesting?" El asked.

Mara gave her a tight smile. "I trust that yer sense of taste is going to be better than mine."

El couldn't help but snort. "Not mine personally, no. I grew up eating pickled fish and lake greens. These are too sweet. But Vorwin—a great cook—and the kids, all say that these will be perfect."

"Huh," was all that Mara said in response.

"What did you grow up eating?" El couldn't help but ask. She was so, *so* curious about Mara, who she was, where she'd come from, why her skin was so golden and perfect.

Mara just shook her head. "Worsen'en you, I reckon. Only thing I like is smoked flavors."

Smoked ice? How would that taste? El would have to ask Vorwin about that.

They went through the contracts, Mara asking questions,

El making changes as they bargained. (Vorwin had been insulted that El insisted on being the one to negotiate, but El refused to let anyone else do this part of the proposal. She alone got to talk with Mara, to hammer out this deal.)

There weren't many changes, just enough for Mara's pride, as she'd said. The contracts weren't finalized yet—Sigder would make clean copies that would have to pass his mother's exacting eye, then all the parties would sign them.

However, they did get everything in place, the menus finalized, the helpful signage preliminary agreed on, after just a short time.

"I'll close the shop for a couple days so ye can come in and paint," Mara suggested.

"Wyne actually suggested a week, if you can afford to stay closed that long. That way, you can build anticipation for the grand re-opening," El told her.

Mara shook her head. "I never woulda thought of that."

"Me neither," El admitted. "While I've been guiding the children as much as I can—so many of the ideas came from them. They have a much better sense of business than I do."

"Blind leading the blind, eh?" Mara teased.

El would not, *would not*, blush again at that. "Hopefully it's better than that."

"Eh, it ain't yer fault. I got no experience either," Mara said rucfully. "Thatur had a good business sense to him. When we first came here, I knew nothing. Not running a shop, or living in a city, or dealing with customers. Not a thing."

"But you've made it this far," El said.

Mara gave her an elegant, one-shouldered shrug. "Barely." She turned and looked at El again, coating her with that warm regard. "I can't thank ye enough for the offer. Even if the shop fails, it's good to have someone to stand with me again. Even just for a while."

El gave her a tight smile. She wanted to tell Mara that she wasn't going anywhere, that she was going to stay right here, and help.

But she couldn't, not in all honestly. Elves lived such long lives. And she'd just arrived there. Her contract was only through the summer. Once it was over, El didn't know what she was going to do. Stay here in the city? Find more work? Or continue to wander? She couldn't honestly say.

Instead, she merely nodded at Mara and let the matter drop.

The rest of her life was surely a matter for another day.

Now, there was work to do.

CHAPTER SIXTEEN

Though El preferred the clean white walls and unadorned spaces of *Ice & Berries*, she had to admit that Sigder's work wasn't half bad.

In fact, it was excellent.

Now, when customers came in, they were directed to the right, where a wall-sized mural explained the process, what Nilafels produced, the concept of pouring flavorings on the ice, with a final image of a young Human boy, a Dwarf, and a female Wood Elf all looking happy and satisfied with their treat.

El hadn't really understood the concept of flow through the store, but seeing it now, it made sense. Customers didn't just wander in, they were directed. Tall wooden poles in sturdy bases, with beautifully dyed blue rope strung between them, created the space for a line.

Mara didn't think that they needed so much crowd control, but Wyne was insistent. "Assume victory," she'd told them more than once.

El tried not to snigger every time she heard that. She figured that it was a phrase from either Ceceline or Gyles.

Sigder had also created the artwork on the brochures that Wyne handed out in the markets, announcing the grand reopening. (Their mother had made the copies for them at a much reduced cost.) El had walked beside her, giving away free samples. While Brytha had discovered the (extremely inexpensive but durable) wooden spoons they could use for the free samples, Kucher had been the one to find the molded leaf cups to hold the ice, that didn't need to be washed but could be thrown away.

El had escorted the children home for the evening, then come back to the shop to spend time finishing the last-minute details with Mara, as she had the last few nights.

When El stepped into the store (she had her own key now) she couldn't help but admire the transformation that had taken place.

While on the one hand, the old shop had had a certain stark elegance.

However, that was out of place with the clients that *Ice & Berries* hoped to sell to. It needed to be a warmer space, where families would be welcome, as well as a space for those with an admitted sweettooth. Various shades of pink now covered the once pristine white walls. The colorful murals told the story of the shop. Menus drawn on the wall behind the counter informed customers of their choices of syrups. While the names were still fanciful, such as "Golden Berry Flowers" or "Skalit Ice Fog," there were also descriptions of the berries used and the flavors to expect.

The tables were still white, the chairs as well. But they stood as a good contrast to the rest of the area.

"In the back!" Mara called out when she heard the front bell ring.

El nodded and walked past the counter, through the door just past Nilafels, and into the kitchen.

She could tell by the number of pots that Mara had stacked beside the sink that Vorwin had been there earlier.

"You wash. I'll dry," El told Mara as she plucked the dishtowel off Mara's shoulder.

"Thank ye," Mara said.

They worked easily together, as if they'd done this many times instead of just a couple. Eventually, Mara cleared the pile of dishes and wiped her own hands on a different towel.

"That's that then," Mara said, looking around.

The kitchen wasn't very large—about a quarter the size of the shop. It was more long and skinny than wide, with a sink with a water pump on one of the short ends, a huge walk-in cooler on the other, and a small stove and counters taking up the long walls. Sigder hadn't painted anything back here, so the walls were still white and clean.

Which honestly, El felt was more appropriate for a kitchen, though Vorwin had grumbled about it, something about beige people.

"Can I make ye some tea?" Mara asked.

"That would be lovely, thank you," El said. They'd shared tea a couple of nights now, letting the quiet of night fill the kitchen and settle them both. They didn't really need words between them, working around each other in a dance, with Mara filling the pot, El getting out the teapot and cups, Mara measuring out the tea while the water warmed.

"Would ye like to come upstairs?" Mara asked while the tea steeped, looking down at the cups and not meeting El's eye.

El felt her eyebrows rise to the top of her forehead. She'd never been upstairs, to the private areas of Mara's store. The shop took up all of the first floor. At the back of the shop was a locked door that held the staircase going up to where Mara lived. Sigder had even put a sign on it that said, "Staff Only! That means you!" when the children had learned where it led.

"If you feel comfortable with that," El said gently. She didn't want to push Mara. The other person still clung to her grief over Thatur's death. And El wasn't certain what she could give Mara in terms of assurances.

Dwarves tended to mate for life. Mara, though not a Dwarf, had probably expected to be with Thatur forever. Elves did as well. Gnomes and Humans, on the other hand, tended to be picky about partners and didn't necessarily make life-long commitments.

Mara merely nodded and handed El a cup once the tea had been steeped, then stepped out of the kitchen, through the shop, and to the locked door.

The staircase was cold, dark, and dusty. As Mara walked up it, low lights came on: gems attached to the walls that glowed with an internal fire when she walked by.

El wasn't positive what exactly she was seeing. Was that magic Mara was performing? Or were the gems specially attuned to her, built by Thatur?

It bothered her that she couldn't tell. Normally, El was excellent at detecting magic.

This was...different.

Not a spell, nothing spoken out loud, but not a cantrip either. At least as far as she could tell.

The space upstairs was much emptier than El had been expecting. A bed covered with a colorful quilt was pushed against the front wall. A hearth took up one of the back corners, with a child-sized rocking chair beside it. It took El a moment to realize that the chair was custom built for a much smaller, stouter person, not necessarily a child. Shelves with a few books and wood-working tools took up one of the walls. A beautifully carved wardrobe stood beside the bed.

However, that was it. No pictures decorated the space. No rugs covered the floor. Unlike the shop below, this place looked barren and empty, not pristine.

"I shoulda thought this through," Mara said after a moment. "There's no place for ye up here."

"I can sit on the floor," El said hurriedly. She didn't want to leave. Not yet.

"All right," Mara said after a moment.

"Please, go sit on the bed," El said, plunking herself down beside it. She managed not to sneeze, though the dust bunnies under the bed as well as the wardrobe appeared to have generated an entire colony.

Mara nodded and sank onto the colorful quilt. They sipped their tea in silence for a few moments, the peace of the night settling in.

"I can't thank ye enough for what ye've done," Mara said after a few moments.

El gave her a soft smile. "The children will expect a return on their investment," she warned.

"I know," Mara said, her smile fleeting. "And I'll make good on it. Do ye really think people will come?"

El shrugged. "We've been at the market telling people about it. And Ceceline has been advertising it at her shop, as well as Nel and Kucher, at the inn. I think Gyles has also taken a handful of the brochures and given them to some of the wine merchants he deals with. So we may get an initial rush. What we'll have to do is to make sure they keep coming back."

"Aye," Mara said, nodding. The children had been adamant about how important repeat business was. They'd discussed loyalty cards—buy twenty ices and get one free sort of thing—but that seemed like too much to offer all at once. They had to get the store re-opened and running smoothly first. It had been four days, and Mara couldn't afford to not have any income for much longer.

El took a sip of her tea. The flavor was smoky, a flavor that Mara had stated she liked. El was getting used to it, as well as the smoked fish that Mara had once shared with her.

"Thatur...I think Thatur would like what we've done," Mara said after a few moments. "I know he always had plans for the shop. But he was so ill, so tired all the time, there wasn't much more he could do."

El nodded. "Tell me about him," she said quietly.

Mara gave her a heartbreaking smile. "Thatur Icemaster was bighearted. Kind. Gruff. He'd hrumph at me but there'd be a twinkle in his eyes when he did it."

El smiled. She'd known a Dwarf or two who'd done the same sort of thing.

"Did ye know that though a Dwarf gets a family name, the ones who are skilled enough earn their own name?" Mara said.

"I did," El said. "Was Icemaster a family name? Or earned?"

"Passed down," Mara said. "He...he was earning his own. Or trying. But the attempt, the accident, well, it cost him his life." She sighed and looked down. "I couldn't help him, at the end."

"I'm sure you did everything you could," El said soothingly. "You got him here, to Osirholm. Had healers look at him, right?"

Mara nodded, still not meeting El's eye. "Aye. But it was too late."

"I'm sorry for your loss," El said simply. She didn't know what else to say.

Mara looked around the room suddenly, as if seeing what else was there, what else they could talk about. "Tomorrow's the big opening, eh?"

"It is," El agreed. "And we've done all we can to make it a big splash."

"Good, good," Mara said. She yawned, then looked horrified. "I'm sorry! I'm sorry! It's just been so long since I've had someone else up here. It...it makes me relax."

"Ah, I see," El said. While she was used to having her own space, her own room, obviously Mara was used to the company of other people.

It amused her how Mara's eyes seemed to be drooping of their own accord.

"Here," El said, standing suddenly and taking Mara's cup.

"Don't go," Mara said, her words sounding naked and afraid.

"I'm not," El assured her. "Not yet. Now, I'm going to sit here while you get yourself ready for bed, then stay with you until you fall asleep."

Mara nodded slowly. It didn't take her long to change into a long sleeping shirt, her auburn hair pulled back into a tight braid for the night.

El retook her spot on the floor while Mara slipped under the quilt. It seemed far too light to El, then again, she preferred sleeping in a very cold room in a bed piled high with blankets.

All the lights in the room suddenly dimmed.

That must have been magic, for Mara to do that, but El still wasn't sure how the other person had done it. She hadn't seen any magic, hadn't felt it.

Who was Mara? Where had she come from? El still didn't have answers to her questions.

Still, after Mara had settled, El started to quietly sing, a lullaby that her own mother had sung to her.

It wasn't a spell. Not really, even though the words were spoken out loud. There might have been a touch of magic woven through the refrains, a soothing of the heart, a calming of the nerves.

Mara proved no more resistant to it than El had been, and was soon breathing heavily, sleep overtaking her.

When El was certain Mara was asleep, she stood again, pausing to look down on the other person.

Even asleep, Mara was ethereally beautiful, her skin with that same golden glow.

The lights dimmed further, heightening the effect.

No, Mara wasn't quite Human, was she? No one Human glowed like that.

El had no problems seeing in the dark, walking through the empty room, down the lightless staircase and out into the shop. The lights there, too, had been turned off. She let herself out and locked the door behind her, making her way through the quiet street.

Maybe sometime Mara would trust El enough with her secret.

In the meanwhile, El needed to get some sleep.

They had a grand opening tomorrow.

Hopefully there would be customers to make it a cele-
bration.

CHAPTER SEVENTEEN

El heard the commotion as she and the kids walked up the small street that held Mara's shop before she saw it.

There appeared to be a large gathering of people in the street.

Wait.

Were those customers? All lined up and ready for the grand opening?

El glanced at Wyne and Sigder. They both grinned up at her.

Seemed that their marketing ploys had worked, at least for the first day.

They hurried up the street, winding through the crowd and letting themselves into the shop.

Mara stood behind the counter, staring at them with big eyes. "There's people," she said in a hoarse voice.

"There are," El said reassuringly. "And that's a good thing."

They quickly set up their stations. Sigder was at the front

door, guiding people into the line and explaining the process. Wyne was behind the counter with Mara, pouring syrups on the bowls of ice that Mara would get from Nilafels. El would float between them, restocking the syrups, clearing tables, washing dishes, and spelling each of them when they needed a break.

It wasn't quite as complicated as the battlefield. Customers, not demons, were about to descend on the store.

Still, El felt her heart start to race when she finally unlocked the door and called out in a cheery voice, "Welcome to *Ice & Berries'* grand reopening, everyone!"

Then the chaos began.

The opening went as smoothly as could be expected, particularly since none of them were used to working with such a large crowd. Fortunately, the customers were understanding and patient. Most of the people were new, and so Sigder's explanations were a big hit. He even started playing a game with those waiting, having people at the front of the line explain things to those people behind them.

El felt like she danced between the tables, smoothly picking up bowls and spoons and depositing them into a large bin. Occasionally she'd have to scrub sticky tables or chairs. Once the bin was full, she'd slip behind the counter to the kitchen and hurriedly wash everything. She also kept Nilafels stocked with water, and Wyne with syrups.

Mara appeared to be in her element, drolly explaining the great machine, the invention of Thatur Icemaster, as well as the various syrups. Wyne did her part, being cute and talking about the health properties of some of the berries and herbs that Vorwin had used.

They finally got a breather just before dinnertime. El escorted the tired children home, then hurried back to the shop to help Mara prepare for the after-dinner rush.

At least after dinner, the line no longer went out the door. Vorwin appeared soon afterward, with three of her cousins in tow. She set them to work immediately, helping El clear tables while she made her way into the kitchen to cook up more syrup.

The four Gnomes were the last to leave, and finally El could close the door, Mara could turn down the lights, and the pair of them could collapse into chairs in the back of the shop.

"My spirits!" Mara cried as she leaned all the way back in her chair, tilting her head back to see the ceiling. "I've never!"

"I know," El said ruefully. "I haven't either." She answered without lifting her head from where it was slumped on her arms folded over the table. "I think Sigder and Wyne have many more ideas now."

"Great," Mara groaned. "I'm a gonna have te hire someone," she added. "I cannot expect ye to come and help all the time."

Mara's Dwarvish accent grew a lot stronger when she was tired, El had realized.

"I can come in the evenings," El said softly, finally finding the strength to sit back in her chair. "If you'd like me to. If you'll have me."

Mara leaned forward in her chair and brought her head down. "I'd like that," she said. For the first time, her amber eyes weren't drowning in sorrow. "Thank ye."

"You're welcome," El said, her smile joyful. "And thank

you for letting Wyne and Sigder try out their ideas for the business."

Mara waved a hand as if to brush that away. "I needed to do something to keep Thatur's dream alive." She looked around the shop appraisingly. "I'll do the rest of the cleaning in the morning," she said. "Right now, I'm gonna drop."

El nodded. "Aye. Me too."

"Still...wouldn't mind a cuppa to settle me," Mara said.

"I agree."

They pushed themselves up to standing, groaning in harmony, then laughing.

It occurred to El that was the first time she'd heard Mara laugh, truly let go.

The sound was sweeter than ice wine.

They went into the kitchen, which Vorwin and her cousins had graciously cleaned. Nothing was put away—pots, spoons, bowls, and other utensils all lined the counters—but everything was clean.

Mara started the tea and El got the cups, the pair of them performing their usual dance.

"Huh," Mara said as she opened the tin holding her favorite smoky tea.

"What is it?" El asked.

"I think...I think there isn't as much in here as there was last night," Mara said, shaking the tin.

"I bet Vorwin took some," El said. "I did tell her that your favorite flavor was smoky."

Mara smiled and shook her head. "Smoked ice, huh?"

El shrugged. "Worth a try."

They finished making the tea and headed upstairs to Mara's bedroom.

El was surprised to find that an additional chair had been

added, something comfortable for her to sit in, next to the bed.

"When did you have time to get this?" El asked. It was simply made from white pine, unadorned, but beautiful.

"I got up early," Mara said, sounding defensive. "I know a shop nearby. They were...they were friends of Thatur's."

"Was it difficult for you to go?" El asked quietly.

Mara's laugh, this time, was shaky and full of pain. "Eh, I should have known ye'd be the one to guess how hard it was. 'Cause it was hard. They don't blame me for Thatur's death. But I do."

El sat in the welcoming chair, taking a sip of her tea. "Tell me what you can," she said softly, indicating that Mara should sit on the bed.

"It's called The Furniture Emporium," Mara said. "Do ye know it?"

El shook her head, understanding that Mara still wasn't really ready to talk much about Thatur, that the other person had deliberately misunderstood her and chosen to talk about that morning instead.

"A big warehouse full of furniture, all made by Dwarven craftsmen and women. I hadn't gone back, since, well," Mara said. She took another sip of her tea. "They were kind to me. Well. Kind in a Dwarven manner."

That made El smile. "Huffing and hrumping at you while still smiling and trying to be welcoming?"

"Yes. That. Exactly." Even in the dim light, El could see Mara rolling her eyes. "They're not sentimental, I guess. Oh, they have great family pride. But Thatur, because he died before he could earn a name, he isn't a hero to them. Only to me."

After the silence ensued for a while, El finally said,

"Thank you for bearing that, those memories, to fetch me this chair."

Mara gave her a quick smile. "I may have been selfish in that."

El merely raised an eyebrow.

"Ye see, ye being here. And yer singing. It brought a peace to me heart," Mara admitted.

"I'm happy to come up here and sing to you every night I work in the shop," El said softly.

"I know," Mara said, nodding. "Yer like Thatur that way. Giving." She paused, looking down at her cup. "I won't take too much this time. I promise," she added, her voice breaking.

"I believe you," El said. "I trust you."

Mara looked up, her eyes suddenly blazing. "Ye shouldn't."

"Why not?"

Mara looked away, then shook her head. "I don't want to tell ye."

"Then don't," El said. She paused, then found herself compelled to say, "Or rather, don't tell me until you're ready."

That got her a nod. They sipped their tea in the quiet, until Mara's head started drooping with tired again.

"Go get ready for bed," El directed as she grabbed the cup from Mara's hands before she fell asleep sitting up.

"Ta," Mara said. It didn't take her long before she'd slid under the covers, the lights suddenly dimming.

Though El had been expecting the change in the lighting, she still didn't see any magic flowing out of Mara.

El sang a different lullaby but it had the same effect: Mara was breathing heavily, sound asleep, after just a few notes.

El sat there for a while, perplexed.

Obviously, something had happened, either to Mara or with Mara and Thatur. Something bad.

El could only wait until Mara decided to trust her enough with the truth.

CHAPTER EIGHTEEN

The next few days flew by in a hurry of business. El worked with the children on their lessons in the morning: maths, language, history. After they ate something for the midday break, they'd walk up to the shop and spend the afternoon working hard, running the shop, dealing with customers. Then El would walk them home, grab a quick bite of dinner, and go back to spend the evening in the shop with Mara.

By the third day, Mara had finally found help—the daughter of one of Thatur's friends who could come by when the shop first opened. As Zuri was a Dwarf, she was best at clearing tables and explaining to customers, not serving, not unless she stood on boxes, which El had been told adamantly was beneath her dignity.

After a day of training Zuri, El and the children went back to their previous routine, spending all day doing classwork. Ceceline appeared to approve of their shift in focus. The children, too, seemed relieved. Running a shop like Mara's took a lot of work, and they were happy for the reprieve.

It made El wonder how Mara was doing, working day after day, if there was some way that El could give her a break.

Mara took matters into her own hands, though, closing the shop for a day the next week, on one of the major Dwarvish holidays. Mara assured El that she wouldn't close for all major holidays, but since Zuri wouldn't be there to help her, it made sense to take a day off. Plus, Mara needed a day's rest.

El still found herself leaving the Margravine's house after dinner. Her room, though a haven of peace, seemed too small that night.

So El decided to go to the market, to check in with Frysa, to see if any progress had been made about the young man using magic to rob people.

The night market sounded as loud as always as El made her way up the street. The smell of meats grilled over open flames filled the air. Though the night itself was cool, humid air carried on the winds as they traveled through the mass of people gathered there.

As usual, El tried something new that night (though still not the fried crickets—she wasn't up for that yet). This time, she got something referred to as a slider. There were three of them on a platter, made up of a small circle of minced meat served on an equally small bun. Each came with its own special sauce. One was too spicy for El (of course) but the other two were deliciously sweet and mild—the honey-mustard being her favorite.

After her snack, El wandered over to where Frysa had her stall. The woman appeared to be doing well, as half her table was sold out already.

She had a new item there, something El hadn't seen

before. It looked like a small, straight stick, the dough tightly curled in around itself, and coated in sugar.

"El! It's good to see you," Frysa called out when El came walking up. "Heard you've been busy at *Ice & Berries*. Sorry I haven't been able to stop by."

"I understand," El said. She'd had more than one person apologize to her for not yet making it to the shop. However, she also knew that people were busy.

"What are these?" El asked, pointing to the sticks.

"Cinnamon stick cookies," Frysa said. At El's blank look she explained, "They're baked dough that's been twisted with cinnamon, then rolled in sugar. They're crunchy and sweet. Try one!"

El hesitated. She didn't want to take advantage of Frysa by getting a free sample. On the other hand, those sticks gave her an idea.

Though Frysa had said the sticks were crunchy, El hadn't appreciated just how crunchy they were. It bit off hard, but then she felt the butter and sweetness on her tongue.

"These are amazing!" El said. "They'd go perfect with ice."

"Uhm, okay?" Frysa said, unsure what El meant.

El could see it already. A larger bowl of ice with sweet syrup poured on it, with two of these cinnamon stick cookies sticking out of the side. It could be a more expensive, more extravagant treat. Maybe something big enough for people to share.

"I'd like a dozen, please," El said, reaching for her pouch.

Frysa got a stubborn look to her. "Why do you think your money is any good here?"

El grinned. "Because I'm going to be taking these to my team, to see if maybe we can get develop a dish that features these. If we can, then I'm going to come back and bargain with you about wholesale prices. You need to charge me now, so I'll have an idea of how much I should be looking to spend if Mara and the others decide they like them."

"Oh," Frysa said, blinking in surprise. "Yes, that actually makes sense."

El couldn't help but be pleased with herself and her slowly accumulating business knowledge.

She explained her concept to Frysa, whose eyes suddenly widened. "Oh! I know exactly where you should go!"

Frysa gave El some basic instructions how to get to a different stall in the market, involving walking along the aisle where the Gnomes had their spread but stopping before she got to the hair dyes.

"There's a sweet shop there. You'll see what I mean," Frysa said, but that was the only clue she gave to El about what she was looking for.

El thanked Frysa and went on her way, wandering around and looking at all the remarkable goods she found there, wondering if she'd ever need even half of it.

The smell of sugar drove her forward, until she found the stall that she thought Frysa had been talking about. Several jars holding sparking decorations lined the top of the stall, with little bowls beside them and a series of tasting spoons.

El had probably walked by this stall before and not realized that the decorations were edible. They came in the same incredible colors that Gnomes sometimes used for their hair, shockingly bright colors. But there were also some metallics —golds and silvers—along with some that were brilliant white.

Mostly, the decorations were just small straight pieces, like thick thread that had been frozen and shattered. The whites and metallics were in different shapes, though, like diamonds and small balls.

The Gnome who ran the stall—a female whose stubby fingers were covered in rings—stayed chatting with her neighbor when El approached the table. She nodded when El held up a tasting spoon, wanting to try the various colors.

To El, they mainly tasted of sugar. Maybe they held some other flavor, but if they did, she couldn't discern it.

"What do you call these?" El asked the Gnome when she finally finished her conversation and came over to chat with El.

"Sprinkles," the Gnome said, "because you sprinkle them on things, like cakes and sweet breads."

Or ices, though El didn't say that out loud.

El bought a bottle of the bright white (because it would look good on red syrup) and a bottle of the silver (because it was pretty and the pieces were in the shapes of snowflakes).

When El showed Frysa her purchases, the woman just chortled. "See! I told you. That shop would be perfect. Though I would have thought you'd go for the bright pink or green."

El hesitated. "Maybe I should have," she said, mournfully looking down. She'd bought the colors that *she* liked, not necessarily what other people might find attractive.

"No, no, I'm sure it's fine," Frysa reassured her. "Besides, if these don't work out, at least you have the concept and can come back to get more. Right?"

"Right," El said, relieved. "Have you had any more problems with that magical thief?"

The way that Frysa's face darkened made El concerned.

"The guards ran into him yesterday. He nearly killed one

of them escaping, burning the poor man but good," Frysa said.

El felt her eyes grow wide. "That's terrible!"

"The guard made it okay, but everyone is now on the lookout for that thief," Frysa said. "That boy was wearing some sort of magical disguise. The guards couldn't see behind the mask, but they could see that the only magic coming from the boy was from around his face and neck. Someone magical feels differently, right?"

"Yes, they do," El said, nodding. How clever for the guards to figure that out! As an Elf, her entire being would feel magical, not just her head.

"But the problem was that he was in Dinkly's Magic Depot when they caught him," Frysa said. "Though stores with magical supplies are supposed to be well protected, there are rumors that some of them are missing stock."

"What kind of stock?" El asked, a cold chill going down her back.

"Special chalk, for doing protection circles," Frysa said. "Quicksilver, and a couple other reagents. Plus a cauldron."

El shook her head slowly. While those components by themselves could mean nothing, they might also add up to someone trying to produce a strong spell.

Quite frankly, something too strong and sophisticated for that boy to be doing.

"Do we know yet where he lives?" El said.

"No one knows," Frysa said. "The guild paid for a wizard to look for him, using the bag that you recovered. But he hadn't owned it long enough, or something, so the wizard couldn't track him. The guards *are* very invested in finding him now, particularly since one of their own has been hurt," Frysa said wryly.

El understood. Of course, the guard would have wanted to do their duty. Especially if the Merchants' Guild was paying them to be vigilant.

One of their own getting hurt, though, would hold their interest for longer.

El walked away from the market, still pondering Frysa's news.

The Elf behind the Great Mistake had started with such simple magical ingredients as well. He didn't have the power of that amulet, the one the boy wore.

El was probably just borrowing trouble. No one would be stupid enough to open up another portal to the demon world, even accidentally.

Would they?

CHAPTER NINETEEN

El shyly presented the cinnamon stick cookies and the sprinkles to Mara the next evening. They'd already met with approval from Vorwin and the kids. It meant a lot to El that she finally might be able to bring her own ideas about the business to Mara.

They spent part of the evening brainstorming how best to serve the cinnamon stick cookies, though eventually, Mara agreed with El that she needed to stock some larger bowls and put a new item on the menu, a "Lovers' Delight" being the proposed name. It would come with two cinnamon stick cookies and lots of sprinkles on top of a cheery red sauce.

El went back to talk with the Dwarf at the sprinkles shop and learned that yes, she could also make hearts. After a little experimentation, they got the right size of sprinkle to put on the ice (not too big that it was overwhelmingly sweet, not too small so that the sprinkles just melted and went unnoticed).

The Lovers' Delight turned out to be a big hit, though it wasn't just couples who ordered it. Sometimes a mother with a group of children would order one, with extra spoons, so that their kids could have something to split between them. Mara and El came up with a couple of different combinations for people to split, including one topped with every color of sprinkle imaginable.

The first month of the store reopening flew by. Mara closed the shop for an afternoon to meet with Wyne and Sigder. They carefully went over the books together, so that Mara could show them her business practices and her profit. While the gross profit was significantly more than what Mara had been making the previous months, the net profit, after she'd extracted expenses like the new bowls, sprinkles, and the cost of the berries, wasn't that large.

Still, Mara had more than enough for rent and food for herself for the next month. The children had a nice lump sum to put into their savings accounts. El then led the group in a discussion of what had gone wrong over the past couple of weeks, what they needed to attend to. The concept of loyalty cards was pushed off for another month—it still felt too soon. Plus, customers appeared to be loyal already, with several regulars who Mara could name.

Wyne looked around the shop, contemplating. "You know, you have a lot of counter space that you aren't using," she said.

"It is being utilized as seating," El pointed out.

"True, but that's just the back of it," Wyne said, nodding. "You could display other foods there. And serve cookies. Or tarts, to keep with the berry theme."

"But I wouldn't be making 'em," Mara pointed out. "I'd need to get a good break to generate a profit."

Sigder nodded. "True," he said. "However, you won't

have as many customers come the rainy season. No one is going to want a cold treat. You might want to start with a few baked items now, to get customers used to the idea, then add more as the weather changes."

El felt her eyebrows rise to the top of her forehead, impressed with the far-thinking that Sigder expressed.

"That could work," Mara said, nodding.

"We should go talk to Frysa," El offered. "She might come up with something you could sell. And she'll probably give you a good deal." She certainly had made the cinnamon stick cookies affordable for them, giving them a good whole-sale price, while still selling them for three to four times that amount at her stall in the marketplace.

"Done," Mara said shyly. She gave El a look that bright-ened her entire day.

The sorrow still burned through Mara's gaze sometimes. However, El thought that the person was finally healing. El expected that Mara would be sad sometimes, and would miss Thatur forever, but the grief no longer filled her entire world.

The change in Mara's mood had also brightened the store. Though Sigder's murals and the change of wall color had warmed up the place, Mara feeling more at peace had also helped tremendously.

After dinner, El collected Mara from the shop, then walked with her to the night market. Mara went immediately to one of the tables that El deliberately ignored, piled high with fried crickets.

"These are so good!" Mara exclaimed after getting a small bag full. "Ye need to try one."

El opened her mouth then closed it again. "Really?"

Mara nodded. "Don't you trust me, lass?" she asked,

smiling slyly. She pulled out a few and tossed them into her mouth, crunching on them. "Nice and smoky."

"Okay," El said. She reluctantly reached out for one and brought it to her nose. It did smell smoky. That was all she could smell. Maybe a bit of salt had been sprinkled on them as well. They felt slightly greasy, probably from the oil they'd been cooked in.

She looked at Mara, who looked expectantly at her, then back at the roasted insect pinched between her fingers.

"Fine," El said.

The cricket actually had very little flavor. It was primarily crunchy, with a touch of smoke and some salt. She wasn't sure about the mouth feel of the sharp insect bits, but it didn't taste bad, at least. It was never going to become one of her favorite foods, but she could see how other people might like them.

They met with Frysa who had some ideas about sweets to serve at the shop, cookies that were drier and would last longer before going bad, something that none of them had thought about.

After wandering the aisles of the night market, El walked Mara back to the shop. They completed their nightly ritual of a cup of tea for each, then headed up to Mara's room above the shop.

"Ye didn't get a share of the profits," Mara said as she settled herself onto her bed.

El shook her head. Though she'd worked in the shop like all of them, it hadn't felt right for her to take any money for it. The ideas were all from the children—all she'd had to do was to check their work. Plus, it had meant for some easy business lessons, which in the end meant less work from her, not more.

"What ye said, when ye came up with all those plans—ye wanted me," Mara said, studiously not looking at El.

"I shouldn't have been so presumptuous," El said. "I just wanted to help you. As I said."

At least this time she didn't feel her cheeks starting to warm.

Yet.

"I'll tell ye my story, if ye want," Mara offered. "For all yer help."

El felt herself grow very still. "Only if you want to," she said softly. "I don't want to make you do something you're still not ready to."

"Eh, if I don't tell ye now, I may lose me courage," Mara said bluntly. She took a deep breath and a fortifying sip of her tea before she started.

"Thatur's family name was Icemaster. He came from a long line of smiths and mages who worked together to create the great ice making war machines, that you Elves use battling the demons up north."

El nodded. She'd surmised that much.

"But Thatur—he was ambitious. He wanted to be more than an Icemaster. He also wanted to master fire."

El found herself suddenly looking at Mara. She didn't say anything though, just willed Mara to continue.

"He was good with fire. Was learning to control it, to weave it, to get it to do his bidding. His family told him he needed to study under a master to truly learn fire, but they wouldn't help with the cost. Thatur...Thatur was stubborn. As stubborn as a Dwarf," Mara said with a slight smile.

Then her expression grew bleak. "He was also impatient, which ye cannot be. Not when working with such a vast amount of power."

Mara was quiet for long enough that El finally felt as though she should ask. "What happened?"

"Me," Mara said. "I happened."

"I...I don't understand," El said.

"I weren't born of a woman and a man," Mara explained. "Though I look Human, I'm not. I was born from fire and magic."

"An elemental?" El asked, impressed. To give form to one of the elementals took a lot of skill. And magic. And power...

But. Thatur hadn't survived for long after he'd cast the spell, had he?

Mara shrugged her shoulders. "I don't think I'm an elemental, or rather a full one. If I were a true elemental, I'd still have a great deal of magic, even in this form. But I don't."

For the first time that El could remember, Mara sounded frustrated, as well as angry.

"The best theory his family came up with was that he caught a sliver of an elemental, not a full one. It came at a cost, though."

"That's why you feel guilty for Thatur's death," El said.

"Aye, that's the heart of it," Mara said. "He poured so much power into me, bringing me to life, that he couldn't recover. I took too much."

El wanted to deny it, that Mara wasn't to blame. Thatur had been the one to set himself an impossible task, to learn fire without a master.

At the same time, she knew that it took tremendous power to cut off an element from their surroundings. To cast them into a more solid form. Even an earth elemental was perceived as vaporous at best. And only true Master Mages had that level of personal power.

Plus, as he had already mastered ice, he naturally took on the burden of powering the spell himself, instead of using up not only all the magic in the nearby area, but all the lives as well. Or perhaps burning down the entire town where they were living.

"When I became aware, when I stepped out of the fire, off the hearth, it took me a while to understand what had happened. I couldn't push what I had of his life essence back into him," Mara said. She sounded ready to weep. "He was my creator. And I killed him."

"It was his choice," El said firmly. "He could have gone to a master. Could have become an apprentice. Could have learned how much power he really needed to master fire."

Mara gave El a wobbly smile. "I know. That's what all his relatives said to me too. They dinna blame me. But Thatur was still proud. Didn't want to make me beholden to his kin. So we came to the city. He opened this shop for me, made me a machine that I could use, to create a product I could sell. It was all he knew, and he gave me that."

"He wanted you, his creation, to live on," El said, "and to carry on his memory." El knew that from heavy experience, from growing up in the war.

"Aye," Mara said. "Which is why I kept trying. Kept going. Even after his death, after he was gone."

A selfish part of El was actually glad to learn that Thatur had been Mara's creator.

Not her mate.

It meant that Mara might *possibly* be open to a relationship...once she finally recovered sufficiently from her grief.

"Thank you for telling me," El said. "I had no idea that was your story." It did explain the other person's glow. And why she always felt warm to El.

Fire made flesh. Not a full elemental, but just a piece of one.

Mara gave a sharp nod. "There. That's me story. I figure that's a good enough payment for helping me. And thank ye. For all ye've done."

The finality of her words struck El. "Wait, do you think I'm going to leave now? Leave you alone?"

Mara blinked. "Yes?"

El gave her a warm smile. "You've told me your history. I know you blame yourself for what happened to Thatur—I would too, if I were in your shoes—but I also know that Thatur was equally to blame. For not being a full Fire Mage before he tried that spell. However, you need to know that I still want to be here, still want to work with you."

"Ye sure?" Mara said. "I'm selfish."

"No, you're not," El said. "You allowed the children to help you. You're contributing to their education. You're letting them try things out in your shop. And you're paying them for it. A selfish person wouldn't do that."

Mara looked away. "I wanted to live," she breathed out. "Those first few moments, when I became aware of the fire and me, when I realized that I wasn't the fire, or not just the fire. That I was separate. I could have stopped myself from grabbing at Thatur's magic. But I pulled hard when it reached out for me. Let it draw me out. Wouldn't let go."

"Did you understand the consequences? You weren't a Dwarf, or a Human. Did you know that you'd kill him?"

"I...Maybe? Those first few moments are still a blur. If only I could have stopped myself," Mara said.

"You didn't know," El said firmly. She'd never worked with an elemental, but she'd heard histories about them, and had at least a vague understanding of how they worked. "You started as a being of pure power. Not of consciousness."

Mara didn't look convinced.

El wasn't worried.

She had all the time she wanted, now, to make sure that Mara understood just how special she was.

Even if it took El the rest of her very long life.

CHAPTER TWENTY

Less than a week later, El was working in the shop after dinner. The first rush was over, but they both expected the second rush to start at any time. El took a break back in the kitchen, washing all the bowls and utensils so that they'd be ready.

When she came back out into the shop, a young man was chatting to Mara. She was about to hand him a sample of one of their more popular flavors, "Summer Mountain Berry," which was made from blackberries, raspberries, strawberries, and a touch of thyme.

"Could I get a bigger sample, please?" the man asked pleasantly.

El had her back to Mara, as she was stocking dishes in the cabinets behind the font counter. So she didn't see any magic being cast, just felt the very familiar wave that cascaded over Mara and herself.

"Eh, ye get what everyone gets," Mara said.

That surprised El. Most people would have caved instantly under such a magical compulsion.

Seemed that Mara might be immune to magic, something she needed to be aware of.

Another wave of magic made El grit her teeth as the young man wheedled. "Please?"

She knew, *knew* that the young man was the same as the one she'd seen in the market. The one who'd hurt one of the guards.

She also knew that she couldn't stop him. He was stronger than she was magically, not if she wanted to stay within the bounds of the King's Law.

"No," Mara said, starting to sound cross.

El silently cheered her on.

"Fine," the young man said. "Then I guess I won't be bothering to buy anything if you have so little concern for your customers."

He turned and flounced out of the shop.

El stood and quickly whispered in Mara's ear. "Close up. Now. In case he comes back. I need to follow him."

Then she raced to the door, casting a quick cantrip to silence the bell as she slipped out.

The young man was still visible to El, walking down the small side street, back toward the main street. She followed at a distance, silencing her footsteps. It wasn't late enough to be full night. She blended with the shadows as well as she could. An Umber Elf would have been completely undetectable, as shadows and dark were the primary elements they worked with.

El worked with ice, and there wasn't a handy snowstorm on the horizon.

Still, El didn't think the young man realized he was being followed. He walked too casually, peering in windows and walking around a clump of teens chatting madly with one another and obliviously taking up the entire boardwalk.

The young man skipped down a staircase built for Dwarves and other shorter beings, having walked past the staircase that was Human-scale.

Huh. Was that one of the ways he was avoiding the guard? By sticking to areas that weren't necessarily built for him?

El grimaced as she walked down, the treads uncomfortable to trod along, being too narrow as well as too short. She took the stairs two or three at a time for the sake of her knees.

When she got to the bottom, she looked around worried. Crap.

Had she lost him? She hadn't spent a lot of time down here on the second tier, just one up from the harbor piers.

Then a familiar blast of magic tugged at her awareness.

There, to the right.

The young man had just used his magic again. El wasn't close enough to see what he'd done, but she had the impression that he'd just pushed an old man with a cane off the boardwalk and into the street instead of walking around him.

El wanted to rush to the old man, to make sure that he was all right.

However, the young man might have done that on purpose, to make sure that no one was following him.

Besides, someone else was there already, helping the old man to stand again.

El determinedly hurried on, keeping the young man just in sight.

It was harder than tracking a demon. They left a huge swath of destruction in their path. Demons weren't subtle.

And while the young man was feeling secure in his

power, pushing yet another person to the side, he wasn't as obvious. El had to keep all her senses tuned forward, to make sure she didn't lose him.

The young man turned down the next street. It held a fair number of taverns with a few boarding houses sandwiched between them. The customers stood outside the doors, loud and boisterous.

El realized that the boy was heading toward an area of Osirholm referred to as "Tangle Town." The streets followed what had once been a creek going through the area, and houses had been dug far back into the hill.

El had never been to this part of Osirholm. There were fewer street lights, which actually made it easier for her to hide, particularly as the night gained more of a foothold.

What little light there was showed just how run down the neighborhood was. Trash had crept up and threatened to overtake what appeared to be an abandoned house. El heard rats scurrying, though she didn't see them. The smell of rotten fruit and bodies that had long since abandoned bathing filled what had been sweet night air as they drew inland, away from the breezes that came from the water. A few people quickly walked by, their heads down, minding their own business.

Had she been spotted? El couldn't be certain.

All she did know was that in front of her, magic suddenly surged. A fireball appeared out of nowhere, directed at her head. The other people on the boardwalk didn't scream, but did start running away.

El couldn't just duck and let it sail over her. The houses directly behind her were all made of wood. Old wood, that hadn't been taken care of or treated well.

Wood that would burn at the slightest hint of a match.

She dispelled the magic—a minor cantrip, honestly—causing the fireball to collapse in on itself. Only a few sparks hissed as they fell harmlessly to the ground.

When she looked up, she couldn't see the young man anymore. Couldn't feel him or his magic. Either he had an incredibly effective invisibility spell that she couldn't detect, or when she'd been distracted, he'd run, fast and far.

Either way, he was gone now.

El paused, looking up and down the street at the various houses. Most of them were some sort of boarding house, where many people lived together.

Did the young man live here, somewhere down this street? Or in this neighborhood? It would be a good place to hide, as it would take the guard forever to question everyone about him.

If the people in this neighborhood would even talk with the guard.

With a sigh, El turned around and trudged back to the main street. She turned around now and again, casting her senses out, seeing if she was being followed.

As far as she could tell, no one paid any attention to her.

El walked back to the night market first, as that was one place where she knew she could find guards who would believe her, who would know something of what was happening. She explained what had happened, and where she'd been.

She didn't have proof that was where the young man lived, but she had a suspicion that his home wasn't far from the place where she'd dispersed the fireball.

Then she hurried back to the shop.

All the lights were off. El let herself in, calling out, "Hello?" as she turned and locked the door behind her.

Mara suddenly appeared. She glowed, like a lantern that had just been uncovered.

El smiled at her. "Are you all right?"

"I'm fine, lass," Mara said, dismissing El's worries with a gesture. "What happened? Why did ye leave that way?"

"Let's make some tea," El said. She led the other person back to the kitchen. With a wave of her hand, Mara turned on the lights, the glowing crystals on the walls suddenly filled with flames.

Huh. El still couldn't feel any magic from Mara. Was that something to do with her elemental nature? That as she was from fire, controlling it took no magic? Not even a cantrip?

As they made tea, El told Mara about the young man, how he'd been stealing from the market, how he'd attacked one of the guard, how she'd tracked him and lost him.

"What do you think he's trying to do?" Mara asked.

"Nothing good," El said. "I'm afraid that now since he's stolen some spell ingredients, that he's going to try some magic that's far beyond him."

Mara shrugged. "Won't that just kill 'im?"

El nodded slowly. "Only in the best-case scenario." Like how Thatur had died from the fire spell he'd tried.

"And in the worst case?"

"He takes the world down with him."

CHAPTER TWENTY-ONE

El put aside the history book that she'd been planning to use for that afternoon's lessons. While it contains some of the pertinent facts, it was also missing a lot of the details.

Besides, this was something that Ceceline had specifically asked El to teach to the children, about the Ice Elves and their lives.

She couldn't do that, though, without touching on magic.

As well as the Great Mistake.

The children came in after lunch, still sluggish from their meal. They complained that they were both too old for a nap, even though many people slept in the middle of the day, when it was hottest.

El would have preferred teaching this lesson in the winter, when it was cold, and perhaps the chill would penetrate the skin of her listeners, letting them feel their subject, and not just hear about it.

Still, El made the best of what she had. She let her magic seep out, into the smooth stones of the floor and up the walls, until the classroom was as cold as the storage room Vorwin used to preserve her meats.

The children perked up as they felt the chill settle in, their minds trying to catch up with what their bodies were feeling.

"I was raised in the north," El started out. "Your mother wants me to teach you of my people, the Ice Elves."

The children looked at each other, then each sat up straighter in their chairs. "Are you doing magic for us?" Sigder breathed out.

El merely chuckled in an attempt to keep the bitterness out of her tone. "No, not really," she said, holding up her bare wrist. "I wear no Mage Mark. I cannot perform big spells, with complicated magic, like a seeing spell, that would enable you to look at visions from the north. What I can do is to chill this area down, to make it seem more like we're there in the north, though only for a while. It is a natural thing for my kind."

"Oh," the children said. They'd known about El's lack of a Mark before, but perhaps it hadn't really sunk in.

So El told them about the ice caves where she'd grown up, fishing in the frozen streams with her mother, pickling lake greens with her father, building snow forts instead of sand castles.

"Even though I was a child, I still knew there was a war going on," El continued. "In the marketplace, there were memory tables, places where people sought out mementos to give to the people fighting, or flowers that would express the grief for the family members they'd lost." El sighed. "On the full moon of every month I'd attend memorial services, remembering the fallen. I'd go with my father to his sister's house, to grieve over the loss of my uncle. So the war was never far away."

Sigder and Wyne at least looked interested, though they'd never known what she was talking about, had never lived in a place grieving for its own.

"Do you know what started the war with the ice demons?" El asked. "Back, five hundred years ago, now?"

The children nodded. "An Elf cast a spell, opened the portals," Wyne said.

"Close, but not really accurate," El said. "Yes, an Elf cast a spell. Belodel Maeglal, may his name forever be cursed."

The children looked surprised. Perhaps his name wasn't always spoken of with such derision down here.

"He was an Ice Elf without a Mage Mark. He thought he knew what he was doing." El shook her head. "Speculation is that he was trying to open up a portal to travel to somewhere else on Annund, to leave the north and instantly arrive elsewhere."

"Is that even possible?" Wyne asked.

"Of course it is," Sigder said. "Isn't it?" he said after a moment, looking at El. "I mean, I've read stories about it..."

"It isn't possible," El said firmly. Or at least that was what the Ice Elves taught.

Could someone master such a spell? Like, perhaps, a dragon? As far as anyone knew the spell was pure fantasy, but there was also a lot of speculation as to why Belodel thought he could do it.

"Oh. Okay," Sigder said.

Wyne had a look of superiority, her entire posture screaming, *I told you so.*

However, El wouldn't be distracted from her lesson.

"There are generally only two ways to power a spell, particularly something as big as what Belodel the Traitor was trying. One is through your own magic. That's a large part of the training you need to become a true Mage, that understanding of what you can and cannot do with your own power.

"The other way is to use the power in your surroundings. Now, some big spells use both. It's why spells frequently require ingredients—"

"Like special chalk, or rare stones," Sigder interrupted.

"Yes, exactly," El said. "Those get used up first, then the Mage has to step up and power the spell on their own. A true Mage can create complex, immense spells, regardless of their own individual power, because of this understanding, this knowledge of what they need to bolster in themselves, and exactly which ingredients to use."

The children nodded, though El suspected this was all new information for them.

"Belodel the Traitor had just enough training, just enough knowledge, to start the spell. What he didn't anticipate was that the demons would be waiting for him. They hijacked his spell, turning it into a portal spell that they could use. They drained him of his life, his magic, to keep the spell running."

The elders speculated that one of the reasons why fewer and fewer demons were coming through the portals was because the life essence of Belodel was finally running out.

"This is why the King's Law came into being," El stated firmly. "You cannot do magic, spells that are spoken out loud or require ingredients, without a Mage Mark. They never want to risk another traitor, who thinks they can do the impossible, and instead, turns the world upside down."

"Did you fight in the war?" Sigder asked.

El shrugged. "Everyone either fights in the war, or contributes to the war effort, in some way or another. The Dwarves provide the war machines. The Humans contribute food. The Gnomes offer strategy, though frequently, they also give us the ingredients needed for spells. The Elves, we fight. All of the different types of Elves contribute fighters for the cause."

The less of the politics involved, and why it was mainly the Ice Elves fighting and not the Wood or Umber Elves, the better.

"Just this one guy, Belodel, caused all this?" Wyne said.

El nodded. "It's why no honorable person would try to do a spell that they hadn't practice, hadn't thought out, hadn't spent months developing. There's always the fear of another Great Mistake."

"Why not just ban magic altogether?" Sigder asked.

El's smile was brittle. "I *am* magic," she said. "Would you ban me? All Elves, Dwarves, Gnomes, and other beings? What about the dragons? Or the other folk?"

The children nodded solemnly, obviously never having thought of such things before.

"No, the Mage Marks were the best compromise that everyone could agree on. Cantrips are allowed, like me cooling off this room. Spells that are spoken out loud, or that use ingredients, are not." It wasn't that complicated when you got down into the details.

"Couldn't a Mage make another Great Mistake?" Wyne mused.

"Their training isn't supposed to allow it," El said. That was what had happened to Thatur. He was already an Ice Mage before he'd tried to master fire. So the spell that created Mara had taken his life.

Still. Idiots abounded. There were always stories about mistakes that even Mages made. Monsters created, towns decimated. Nothing on the scale of the Great Mistake, though.

"I know that neither of you have magic, not really," El said softly. She could see that clearly. They were Human.

"That's what Dad says," Sigder grumped.

"He's right," El said. "Could you learn to cast magic? Perhaps."

She didn't like the way Sigder brightened up at that.

"However, you'd never be able to do powerful spells. You might not even be able to do many cantrips. You might have to study for your entire life just to light a candle from your fingertip."

"Really?" Wyne said. "But in the stories—"

"There's a reason they're called stories," El said gently. "Chances are, you don't have some special magical ability. Beyond what you already have."

"But you just said that we have no magic," Sigder said, determined to be cross with her.

"You have a special eye when it comes to drawings and art," El said gently. "And the gift of tongues. Both of those are their own type of magic, that not everyone can do."

Honestly, Sigder was getting close to fluent in High Elvish, as well as Dwarven. She'd started adding in some Gnomish lessons, which Sigder soaked up like a sponge. El had already recommended getting a tutor for Gnomish for the boy for the next year, as he was quickly outstripping her own knowledge of the language.

"And me?" Wyne said, challenging El.

"You have the gift of numbers," El said. "You'll soon be able to negotiate with anyone for anything."

She sometimes wondered about the path the children would take, and if they'd stick with what their parent had in mind or strike out on their own.

"So while you don't have the magic I do, or the ability to do cantrips naturally, you do have your own gifts. What you do with them, whether you use your powers for good or evil, is up to you."

The children sat for a moment, each contemplating their future for a bit.

"Who wants an ice?" El finally asked to break their deep thoughts.

They all rushed out the door, back into the heat of the day, as the classroom regained its warmth.

CHAPTER TWENTY-TWO

It was after dinner, and El was making her way back up to the shop. Two months had flown by since she'd first arrived in Osirholm. She only had one month left with the Margravines. What was she going to do when her time as a tutor came to an end?

The air seemed more hot and humid than usual. El felt as though she needed to use more of her innate power to keep herself cool. The children had told her that there would be summer monsoons soon, though they wouldn't last for long, only a few weeks at most. Then there would be another spate of summer, before fall arrived and temperatures started cooling off.

Mara had started selling cookies baked by Frysa, either plain or topped with frosting and sprinkles. As she appeared to be selling an equal amount of each, she was planning on adding a third cookie to the menu next.

El paused just outside the door of the shop, looking over her shoulder. No one had seen the young man in the last couple of weeks, though she'd heard from Frysa that more magical ingredients had gone missing.

What exactly was the young man planning? He bore no Mage Mark.

She knew it would be disastrous, whatever it was.

El remained on edge all night at the shop. She didn't snap at any customers, or even at Mara, but only through tremendous self-control (and disappearing into the kitchen to silently scream a couple of time).

When the shop finally closed, the first thing Mara did was lean against the counter, arms crossed over her chest, and ask, "What's wrong with ye tonight?"

El shook her head. "I don't know," she said honestly. "There's just something in the air."

"Rain fever," Mara said with a sly smile. "Happens to everyone. Yer knowing the rain is coming, but the not knowing when is killing ye."

El frowned and shook her head. "I don't think that's it. Though I do have this feeling of...anticipation. Maybe dread?"

Mara just nodded, letting El work it out for herself.

"Maybe it's because it's been sunny all the time. For months now. No rain. No snow. Nothing but sunshine and nice days." El heard the words coming out of her mouth and slapped both her palms over her face.

"Aye, it's so horrible having so many nice days," Mara said dryly.

El sighed as she pulled her hands down. "Okay. So maybe it is the rain, or lack thereof."

"Ye'll get used to it," Mara said.

El took a deep breath and released it, trying to relax her shoulders.

Wait.

She took in another breath.

Was that smoke?

She glanced around the store, but nothing burned in there.

Throwing the front door open, she could smell the smoke more strongly.

"There's a fire," El threw over her shoulder. She took a step into the street.

The feeling of despair that had been sticking to her like a fine mist suddenly drenched her.

That wasn't a regular fire.

"There's magic," El said. "I have to go help. Stay here and protect the shop."

"How?" she heard Mara ask as she flitted down the street.

She sighed and shook her head. Now that Mara had told of her origins, El frequently saw how frustrated Mara was with her lack of magic. She should have been a full fire elemental and able to stand on her own.

However, that was a problem for another day.

For now, El had to find the source of the magical fire.

She let her senses lead her instead of trying to follow her eyes or her nose. It wasn't a spell, but it was a kind of magic, the sort used to find demons hiding in a blizzard.

She raced down the nearest staircase—luckily the one built to Human scale—and then down the main street.

No one was screaming in panic or running away.

Maybe the fire was already contained?

Unsurprisingly, she found herself turning down the same small street she'd been down a couple of weeks ago, into "Tangle Town," where she'd followed the young man with the magical amulet.

Dread filled the pit of her stomach as she hurried along.

Magic grew thicker, as though the humid, still air had trapped it.

She turned a corner and came to a full stop.

Crap.

Did no one else notice the weird green glow of that house on the next block?

Then again, El was one of the few people she knew who'd been trained to see magic. She didn't have to cast a spell to do it, unlike the Human guards.

When the color abruptly changed from green to red, El started shouting at the people who still ambled casually along the sidewalk.

"Run! Run!"

No one paid any attention to her.

Until the roof of the house blew.

Now, screams filled the air. The heavy smoke that El had been anticipating bellowed out. Flames reached for the sky.

As bad as a fire would be in this part of town, where everything was built of old wood, that wasn't what scared El the most.

No, she saved her terror for the creature who shouldered its way out of the house, not merely breaking through the door but tearing off the entire front of the two-story building.

Not an ice demon, but a fire demon.

It had the head of a goat, with twisting horns jutting out of its head and a fire-breathing snout. Two solid legs held up its massive body. Muscles rippled across its broad chest as it swung its arms, punching the few remains of the building it had escaped from.

Like an ice demon, instead of wings it grew a mass of

tentacles, though these threw sparks and would cause more fires. Razor sharp spikes adorned its tail, strong enough to casually destroy the building next to it when it thwacked it.

A brilliantly lit amulet strung around its neck flared, making El glance away. When she looked back, she could see that it had cracked, its power greedily sucked up by the monster.

In an instant, El knew what the young man had tried to do.

He'd tried to permanently change his form so he would no longer be recognized, no longer have to wear some sort of disguise to just walk around Osirholm.

He'd lost control of the spell, though. And a demon had stepped in to "help."

Now, the demon had taken over the young man. Probably killed him, subsuming his lifeforce, just as it had sucked away all the power of the amulet.

Making itself stronger.

El had no spell ingredients. Nothing prepared to fight such a monster.

Besides, she was used to snow and ice, not fire and smoke.

"I'll distract the beastie," said a calm voice from beside her. "But ye'll need to figure out how to stomp 'im."

Mara stood beside her, glowing with her own internal fires.

"Don't—wait—stop—it'll kill you!" El shouted as the other person started walking forward.

Mara threw a grin over her shoulder. "It can try," she assured El.

Was Mara immune to flames as well as magic? El didn't know, and didn't think this was the best way to find out.

She couldn't stop the other person from walking forward

though. Not when the demon howled so loudly it froze her in her tracks, spewing dangerous smoke that made her cough and her eyes water.

What could she do to stop it? What magic did she have, spells that were easy to call?

She couldn't create any kind of useful barrier. That would merely hold it, not stop it.

She had no weapon, nor the time to enchant one, to make it invulnerable to the heat coming off in the monster in waves.

She couldn't make it snow. Not here. Not now. It was too hot. Too muggy.

El looked up. Those *were* storm clouds overhead.

Could she make it rain?

El feared making it worse, that somehow, she'd twist the weather into an attack, or that the rain would never stop.

She wasn't an Ice Mage. Just an Ice Elf.

Whose friend? Partner? Love? Had just walked into danger.

She heard Mara shouting at the creature, getting it to stop and look down at her. It lifted one huge, hoofed foot to stomp on her, to put out the light of her friend.

"NO!" El found herself screaming.

She flung her hands up to the clouds above her and began to shout out her spell. She knew she was breaking the King's Law. Elders would bind her magic, take her away, put her in a cold dark cave without the ability to warm herself or to bring light into her world.

Possibly imprisoning her for centuries.

It didn't matter.

She had to stop this thing. If she couldn't save Mara, she had to avenge her.

El felt the spell flow out of her, changing it on the fly, one of the most dangerous things she could have done.

However, she understood the structure of magic. Deeper than she realized. She'd practiced so often when she'd been fighting demons, tweaking spells she'd created with the Ice Mages as they'd been fighting, adjusting to weather and terrain. It had never been new, but it really hadn't always been the same.

She put all of her own considerable magic and life force into the spell, casting it up toward those heavy clouds above her.

The wind picked up. Smoke swirled around her.

A heavy footfall in front of her caused El to take a step back, though she never stopped chanting, never looked away from what she was doing.

"Come 'ere ye stupid beastie," she heard Mara yelling.

A scream echoed in the small street.

Was that Mara? Some innocent bystander? Her own soul?

El poured on the power, even after the first drops struck her upturned face.

She didn't stop until the heavens opened up and sheets of water began streaming down, drenching her and everything in the street.

Her arms shaking, El slowly lowered them.

The demon bellowed, its pain apparent.

El tried to clear her vision, but the rain made it impossible to see what was actually going on.

The shrinking demon rocked hard to one side, trying to lift a foot that now appeared stuck to the street. Its tail lashed out, unable to reach its opponent. Tentacles fizzled instead of sparked, dying in place.

El's world tilted, her vision growing dark. She'd used too much power to stay standing for long. Her own life force was weak.

The last thing she saw another brightly glowing figure, standing in front of the demon, beautifully lit by its fire, taking it all into herself.

Mara.

Then the cold damp night claimed El's consciousness and she slid away.

CHAPTER TWENTY-THREE

The hard surface El laid on puzzled her.

Was she still in the street?

No. It was softer than that.

She opened her eyes to a dimly lit room. Wooden beams covered the flat ceiling. It smelled sweetly of smoke and… berries?

"Eh, had enough beauty sleep?"

El snorted and realized just how much she hurt. "Ow."

Mara was at her side in an instant. "It's all right. Rest. Don't ye try to move."

El nearly nodded but thought better of that. Her lungs ached when she breathed. Every muscle in her body felt as though it had been strained. If a carriage pulled by a foursome of horses had run over her, backed up, then done it again, she probably would have been in less pain.

"What happened?" El said, finding her tongue.

"Ye stopped the beastie," Mara said. Her warm chuckle sent a fission of relaxing warmth through El's aching body. "Well. We did."

El finally found the strength to turn her head and look at the person sitting beside her.

Mara was perched on the chair she'd bought for El. Her warm glow filled the room with light, much brighter than El had ever seen it before.

"What happened?" El repeated. It took a monumental effort, and El was pretty certain that she was going to pass out from exhaustion again after speaking, but she managed to reach a hand out to Mara.

Warm magic brushed up against her skin. So much power that it made her gasp.

"Yer storm broke the demon," Mara said. "It was starting to slip away. But demons are stubborn, ye know? So I helped it along." She gave El a huge grin. "And took its fire."

"Wait. Are you—you're not a demon now, are you?" El said, fear blotting out her pain and exhaustion for a moment. She even managed to lift her head and her aching body partly up, off the bed.

"Oh, no, no, dearie, nothing like that. I just grabbed hold of that fire. That power. Fed me enough to evolve," Mara said. She held up her other hand and a flame erupted from her palm. "I'm no longer a sliver of a fire elemental, but a full one."

"Really?" El said, surprised, pleased, overjoyed.

And exhausted all over again.

"Yes. Now rest. Ye need yer strength," Mara said.

"Osirholm? It's safe? The rains stopped?" El said as she found her eyes closing again.

"It's safe. Ye did good. Not evil, with yer spell. Now sleep."

El found she had no option but to obey, closing her eyes and letting the cool night come and take her again.

The formal inquiry started the next day, while El still lay in Mara's bed, recovering.

An Elvish Elder visited her—an older, elegant Wood Elf dressed in an immaculate green silk robe—listened to her history, then her story, and cleared her of any wrong doing.

"The demon would have destroyed huge swaths of Osirholm," the elder declared, giving El a serene smile. "And you didn't make a mistake with your spell, not even a small one. The rain stopped when you did. You acted correctly, and saved a great number of lives. Technically, you broke the King's Law. But you won't be censured for it."

The elder's proclamation healed El in ways she didn't realize she'd been broken. However, it still wasn't until the next day that she finally had the strength to rise up out of Mara's bed and make her way down the stairs.

More people crowded into the shop than El had ever seen. Not only was every table full, but a line formed out the door. Zuri waltzed between tables, picking up discarded bowls and wiping down the surfaces. Another Dwarf El didn't recognize kept the line entertained. Mara took orders as fast as she could behind the counter, and—was that Frysa? —helped her out there.

The room grew still when customers saw El.

She froze, and not in a good way.

Suddenly, one of the people sitting at a table close to the door stood up and started clapping their hands.

Everyone in the room joined in, giving El a hearty round of applause.

El looked around, not sure what to do.

"All right, all right, stop it you lot," Mara said as she slipped under the counter and over to El, wrapping one warm arm around El's shoulders, leading her to a chair that had cushions piled up on it and a large sign that said RESERVED on the counter in front of it.

Mara slowly lowered El down into the chair, indicating that she just needed to sit there while Mara scooted under the counter again. A few moments later, she placed a large bowl of mushroom soup—one of Vorwin's specialties—with some freshly baked bread, slathered with butter and garlic.

"Eat up," Mara directed El.

El merely nodded, finding that she was, indeed, starving. It had been three days since she'd had much more than water.

The soup disappeared abruptly, as did the bread. El considered asking for seconds when a bowl of thick meat stew landed in front of her. With more bread.

El could hear Vorwin's comments about needing to fatten her up. This time, she was able to eat more slowly and actually savor the food.

"Got room for an ice?" Mara asked as she cleared the bowl.

"Always," El said. "How's Nilafels doing?"

"The beastie's fine," Mara said with a smile. "Now that I have some magic, I can clear her myself."

El nodded, a bit disappointed.

Of course, now that Mara could do things for herself, she didn't really need El anymore.

The ice that Mara brought was a new one that El hadn't tried before. Though the color was a bright red, it wasn't too sweet. There was an underlayer of both smoke and salt that toned it down.

Honestly, it was probably one of the best ices that El had ever had.

People walked by El and told her thank you as they exited the shop. El didn't want to appear ungrateful. However, how much had she actually done? Mara was the one who'd ended the demon for good.

El pushed her dark thoughts away but eventually, she found herself swaying in her seat.

"Back up the stairs with ye," Mara said, coming out from behind the counter and putting an arm around her again before El could faceplant onto the floor.

"I'll be all right," El said.

Mara just clucked her tongue at her. "Maybe I want to help ye," she said softly.

El nodded and let Mara walk her back up the stairs. She leaned into the other person more than she wanted to, being more tired than she wanted to admit.

"Just one more day," El murmured as she laid down. "Then I'll be out of your hair."

"What nonsense are ye talking?" Mara said, standing beside the bed with her fists jammed into her waist. "Oh. Do ye not remember?"

"Huh?" El said, fighting to keep her eyes open.

Mara waved her arm toward the far side of the wardrobe.

El blinked. Her backpack sat there.

"The Margravines, well, they weren't too pleased with ye. Casting magic like ye did. Even if it did save the city," Mara explained.

"Oh," El said. She sighed and sank back into the bed. She did, now, kind of remember Mara saying something like that before. How she always had a place here, with her.

"Now rest. And don't ye worry. It's going to be all right."

El nodded, her eyelids already closing.

She could find other work. Find a new place to live. Find her way again.

She had more friends now to help.

She sternly told herself that it would be all right as she slipped back into the darkness of sleep.

CHAPTER TWENTY-FOUR

El sat up in the bed as Mara came up the stairs, carrying two cups of tea. No noise came from the downstairs, so El assumed that the shop was closed for the night.

"How ye doing?" Mara asked, smiling at El.

The lights in the room all lit, magical flame filling them. The fire in the hearth also suddenly came to life as well. It wasn't bright—just cozy.

"Better," El said. When she'd woken up earlier, she'd found a sandwich waiting for her, along with a serving of a cold, somewhat spicy, tomato soup—another of Vorwin's specialties. The children had been by every day to see her, despite their mother's protests.

"Good," Mara said. She brought over the tea then sat down on the bed beside El.

El stopped herself from immediately leaning toward the other person, getting closer to her warmth.

"Now, I know ye have some questions," Mara said.

"Uhm," El said, not sure what Mara was talking about.

"What are ye going to do now?" Mara asked gently.

"Oh. Yeah. That," El said.

"I have answers," Mara continued. "Yer staying here. With me. Running the shop," she added calmly.

"But you don't need me anymore," El said.

Mara just gave her a look.

El was *not* going to blush. Ice Elves didn't do that.

It was just the warmth from Mara that caused her cheeks to heat up.

Really.

"What ever gave ye that idea?" Mara asked quietly.

"Uhm, you can take care of Nilafels, now," El said. "You have other people running the shop. Despite what the Margravines think of me, you will still have Vorwin's help. And the children will probably also still come."

"That's all true," Mara said, nodding. "And why would ye think I don't want ye in me life?"

Something about how Mara said the words, the tenderness that filled them, gave El a jolt of hope.

"Really?" El said, looking at the other person, this warm, golden, glorious being.

"Really," Mara said.

She plucked the forgotten tea cup from El's hands then leaned in slowly, carefully, to kiss El.

El reached for the warmth that infused her with both hands, determined to never let go.

The monsoon season came and went. Business did go down when it was so wet and cold. El was glad that Mara had already started selling cookies and other treats, expanding her business beyond ices.

Plus, now that Mara had her magic, she could instantly heat up things in the kitchen, and so they talked about providing hot beverages when fall and winter finally arrived. Maybe something chocolatey, with some mint or cherry syrup in it.

When the hot weather came back after the rains stopped, the shop was doubly busy again. El found herself delighted by her days, serving people, gossiping with the regulars, producing sweet treats. The children even came by with their old tutor Finmore, a fussy Human man who nonetheless thanked El for all the work she'd done with the children that summer, praising her in terms of how much they'd learned. He'd already made the Margravines find a language teacher for Sigder, as he'd now outstripped Finmore in that respect.

El's nights were filled with love and warmth. She didn't have to worry about Mara being Human anymore—there was even a chance that the fire elemental would outlive her. No one knew for certain, though. Not even the Elvish elder who came back to try their ices.

A familiar laugh drew El's attention one afternoon as she came into the shop from the back, carrying a full bucket of clean dishes.

There, sitting at a table just inside the door, was her old master, the dragon Azutjengaban. He looked more Human than Elvish that day, with regular ears, brown curly hair, and searing blue eyes. The only thing that declared him as *other* were the two-dozen dragon whiskers that still dangled from his chin.

What was El supposed to do now? Go greet him? Ignore him? Why was he here, so far to the south?

El did *not* want to come out from behind the counter. Her resentment came on thick and heavy.

It wasn't embarrassment that held her in place. No, it was fear of the rage she might rain down on his head.

But unless she wanted to abandon Mara for the rest of the day, she had no choice.

El pasted a smile onto her face, composing her expression into a look of supreme serenity, then stepped onto the floor of the shop.

She started at the back and worked her way toward the front, cleaning up tables and refilling her bucket, ignoring the eyes she felt boring into her.

Azutjengaban sat at the table with two Humans, both wearing rich robes. El could feel the magic they oozed. Mages, she'd bet.

Or other dragons who hid their appearance better.

As El neared the table, Azutjengaban called her over with a wave of his hand.

El set the bin half-full of dishes down on an empty table and walked over to him.

"It's so good to see you doing so well for yourself!" her former Master said.

Sarcasm? Or actual happiness? El wasn't certain.

"Thank you," El said.

"I heard you caused quite a stir down here a few weeks ago," Azutjengaban continued.

"I was cleared of any wrongdoing," El quickly pointed out.

"Oh, I know, I know," Azutjengaban said, nodding. "That spell you managed was quite the treat."

El wasn't exactly sure what to make of that. "I'm glad you approve," she said, her tone with a touch of frost in it.

Azutjengaban grinned at her. "Of course I do! I trained you well."

El forced herself to remain still, to just smile pleasantly, to not roll her eyes at him.

She might pull something if she did.

"I won't be here for more than a day," Azutjengaban continued. "I just wanted to stop by and say hello."

"It's good to see you," El said, the words begrudging though honestly, it did kind of feel nice that he'd look her up.

Azutjengaban and his companions stood to go. El picked up her bucket and watched them.

The dragon stopped at the door after his companions had already gone through.

"I am proud of you," he said softly. "You saved a city with a spell you created on the fly, never having practiced it at all." He waved his hand in the air as he stepped across the threshold.

El nearly dropped the bin she held when magic coursed around her left wrist. With shaking hands she set it back down on the table, then lifted her arm, letting her light robe fall back to expose her wrist.

The wrist that now bore two silver bands.

A Mage Mark.

She looked up at Mara, who nodded at her and gave her a big grin.

El took a deep breath, her own warmth filling her chest.

She'd done it. She was finally an Ice Mage. Able to legally cast spells and make her way through the world.

And not alone.

She smiled back at Mara, the world turning bright and new.

Never alone. Not anymore.

She had her Ice. And her Fire.

And the entire world to explore, with Mara at her side.

READ MORE!

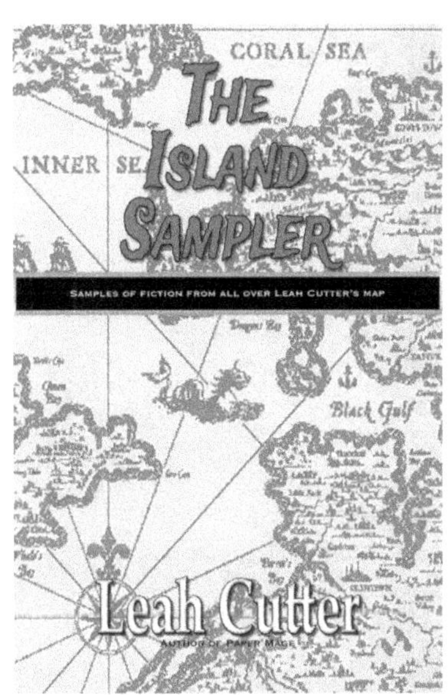

Do you enjoy exploring strange new worlds, new cultures, new people?

Journey into the various lands envisioned by Leah R Cutter.

204

ABOUT THE AUTHOR

Leah Cutter writes page-turning fiction in exotic locations, such as a magical New Orleans, the ancient Orient, Hungary, the Oregon coast, rural Kentucky, Seattle, Minneapolis, and many others.

She writes literary, fantasy, mystery, science fiction, and horror fiction. Her short fiction has been published in magazines like *Alfred Hitchcock's Mystery Magazine* and *Talebones*, anthologies like Fiction River, and on the web. Her long fiction has been published both by New York publishers as well as small presses.

Find Leah's books on Knotted Road Press at (www.KnottedRoadPress.com)

Follow her blog at www.LeahCutter.com.

Reviews

It's true. Reviews help me sell more books. If you've enjoyed this story, please consider leaving a review of it on your favorite site.

Come someplace new...

Are you a traveler? Do you enjoy exploring strange new worlds, new cultures, new people?

Journey into the various lands envisioned by Leah Cutter.

Sign up for my newsletter and I'll start you on your travels with a free copy of my book, *The Island Sampler*.

I will never spam you or use your email for nefarious purposes. You can also unsubscribe at any time.

http://www.LeahCutter.com/newsletter/

ABOUT KNOTTED ROAD
PRESS

Knotted Road Press publishes dynamic fiction set in exotic locations and unique non-fiction voices in genres such as autobiography, business, cookbooks, and how-to. Our authors cover a wide range of genres including science fiction, fantasy, mystery, literary, and poetry, appealing to all readers. We offer both DRM-free ebooks and print books for a global readership.

Knotted Road Press
www.KnottedRoadPress.com
www.KnottedRoadPress.com/Shop